Shadow of the Wendigo

Dale T. Phillips

ISBN: 0615931049
ISBN-13: 978-0615931043

Other works by Dale T. Phillips

The Zack Taylor Mystery Series
A Memory of Grief
A Fall From Grace
A Shadow on the Wall

Story Collections
Apocalypse Tango (Sci-fi, End-of-world)
Fables and Fantasies (Fantasy)
Crooked Paths (Mystery/Crime)
Strange Tales (Magic Realism, Paranormal)
Halls of Horror (Horror)
Jumble Sale (Short Stories)

Non-fiction Career Help
How to Improve Your Interviewing Skills

For more information about the author and his works, go to:
http://www.daletphillips.com

First printing, December, 2013
13579108642

DEDICATION

To the Fergusons: Stephen, Amanda, Lorna, Charlotte, and Heather.
So glad you came and stayed for a time on our side of the pond.

ACKNOWLEDGMENTS

Almost all writers need editors, and a number of people have given feedback on this book, in hopes of making it better. A hearty thank you to Vlad Vaslyn, Stacey Longo Harris, Ursula Wong, and Pete Ewing-- all authors in their own right, who took the time and effort to read this work and offer their suggestions to make it better.

My thanks also to the Tyngsboro Writer's Group, including, but not limited to: Mike Johnson, Joe Ross, Karen Johnson, Brian Hammar, and Bernie Ziegner. And thanks once again to the helpful staff at the Tyngsboro Public Library for giving us space to meet and work.

Many thanks to Loren Coleman: Cryptozoologist, Author, Documentary Consultant, and Director of the International Cryptozoology Museum, Portland, Maine. One of the coolest jobs in the world. Stop by the museum next time you're in Portland, and he can explain the differences between Yetis, Sasquatches, and skunk apes.

As always, thanks to my wonderful family: Mindy, Bridget, and Erin, for suffering my peculiar and solitary profession of writing.

To my dear and supportive friends and loved ones for making things more enjoyable along the path of life.

To all those who have helped teach me to write, through their works.

And to you, dear reader, my heartfelt thanks, for reading this one.

Feel free to contact me and let me know what you thought of the book and what it's about.

Whoever battles monsters should take care not to become a monster too,

for if you stare long enough into the Abyss, the Abyss stares also into you."

— Friedrich Nietzsche, Beyond Good and Evil.

CONTENTS

PROLOGUE

Sean Laporte snapped out of the dream with a start, shivering and confused.

Ree turned on the bedside light, rubbing her eyes. "What is it?"

"I was walking through snow in a forest. I was after something, or it was after me. It was cold, and I couldn't move fast enough."

"Just a dream, right?" Ree said, patting his arm. "Not one of your visions? I'm not marrying a crazy man." She smiled.

"It felt like there was something important I had to do."

"Go back to sleep."

Sean got up. "In a bit. I'm okay," he lied, the feeling of dread still with him. "You go back to sleep."

"'K." Ree switched the light off, and Sean padded out to the living room, wearing only his boxer shorts. He peeked through the curtains, but all was dark outside. He wanted to go get his service automatic from the bedroom closet, but resisted the urge. Ree would hear him, and wonder why he wanted a gun in the middle of the night. And he didn't know himself. Perhaps he just wanted the reassuring heft of a weapon.

For something had disturbed the peace of night, and Sean couldn't quite put a name to the feeling. But whatever the disruption of his rest was, somehow he knew it was dangerous.

PART I

CHAPTER 1

Jimmy Whitefeather knew his time was up. Getting caught out here in the forest could be fatal. All he wanted was to get back to his cabin before the storm hit. He scowled at the first flakes of snow spitting down from the lead-colored sky.

In the ghostly silence of the Ontario wilderness, Whitefeather was the only thing that could be seen moving in the vast landscape. His snowshoes kicked up puffs from the smothering layers of fallen snow. Every other living thing was burrowed down against the oncoming storm, another of the many that had lashed the region. The wind was a malign entity that had joined forces with the cold, making relentless foes against the living.

Whitefeather was out checking his traps, but so far had nothing for his labors. In times past, the people of the land had revered the ancient ways, and respected the spirit of each animal. If an animal must be killed, pardon was first asked. But Whitefeather was a modern man, and never apologized to the spirit of any creature that fell to his trap or gun.

To Whitefeather, food was food, whether it was an animal he caught, or the canned goods that helped he and his wife Sue get through the winter. It had been a harsh season, a scant harvest of food and pelts from his traps. So he had been out longer than he should have, with a storm on the way. He was hungry now, after long hours of cold and exertion, and craved the hot food Sue would have waiting for him.

As he approached the uprooted log that served as his marker, Whitefeather saw that the trap had been sprung. He smiled and unslung the rifle case from over his shoulder, resting it against the log. His smile disappeared when he squatted to inspect his catch. The dead rabbit caught in the steel teeth was emaciated from hunger, it's fur patchy and damaged.

Whitefeather wrenched the carcass free. Bits of flesh and fur clung to the teeth, as if the trap was reluctant to part with its prey. He stood and hefted the corpse for a moment, the meager reward for all his extra effort and risk. He should have kept it, shabby as it was, but he cocked his arm and hurled the dead rabbit into the forest. The body spun until it struck a tree, and rebounded to land in the snow. Lifeless eyes stared up at the pitiless, surrounding trees.

There was no time to clean and reset the trap. Very well, he'd get it the next time. Whitefeather picked up his rifle case and looped the strap over his shoulder. He looked up at the sky once more, gauging. Hard-driving flakes pelted his face, stinging his eyes. He brushed the snow away and struck out for home.

He moved with the pace of the experienced snowshoer, a smooth, steady rhythm that covered ground quickly. The wind picked up, hurtling straight at him. Each puff of snow kicked up by his snowshoes was quickly whisked away, as if by a tidy, unseen butler, and his tracks were wiped out as soon as he made them. The snow blew into his eyes, making it hard to see, but he knew the way home and maintained his pace.

Whitefeather thought he heard a moan. He stopped and cocked his head to listen, but the only sound was the crackle of wind-driven snow against the hood of his parka. Whitefeather shook his head in frustration and continued on. Racing the storm, he had no time for odd sounds or idle fancies. He spat, as if to purge himself of his folly, his cheeks stiff from the cold.

The snow blew into large drifts, and slapped against Whitefeather like cold waves. Despite his effort and his warm clothing, he felt chilled. He tried to huddle further into his parka, cursing.

Another odd sound skimmed by, making him stop again. It had seemed like a high-pitched wail, but had been so short and faint that Whitefeather wasn't sure if he had imagined it. Either the wind was playing tricks on his hearing, or there was something strange going on. His ever-quick temper rose again. He did not have much imagination, and he hated mysteries.

Whitefeather resumed the homeward trek, but over his anger, a feeling of dread crept up on him. Something was wrong in the forest, the familiar place. As his certainty and self-confidence slowly crumbled, he moved faster, spurred by a nameless fear.

Whitefeather heard a high, clear cry and felt a chill far colder than the wind. It wasn't like the howl of a wolf or the lonely cry of the loon, but it possessed the eerie qualities of both. He knew every sound in this forest, but this was one he had never heard.

Whitefeather fought down the fear and stumbled forward on watery legs. He willed himself to keep going, for to panic would be to surrender to the storm, and to death. Half-forgotten stories and old legends tugged at his consciousness. The more he tried to push them down, the more persistently they came bobbing back. Elusive bits and pieces of memory flickered back from the time when he was a boy, and afraid of such things. He licked his cold lips and unslung his rifle.

Whitefeather slowed his pace for a time, watching both sides of the trail, every bush and tree a phantom lying in wait.

But the light was too quickly being stolen from the sky. Whitefeather swallowed and wiped fresh sweat from his brow. Now that he was close to his cabin, he picked up the pace again, sacrificing all for the sake of speed. Adrenaline sang through him, and he felt his heart respond with a vigorous pumping.

When the cry came again, he snapped his head up. The wind blinded him with a stinging slap of pellets, and he snagged a snowshoe on a partially submerged bush. He fell, his ankle twisting painfully.

Whitefeather pulled free of the bush with an effort, and groaned at the bolt of pain. He rolled to a sitting position, hissing through clenched teeth. He brushed the snow from his upper body, and leaned over to undo the bindings from his snowshoe. They were stiff, and would not yield to his gloved hands.

Whitefeather cursed and used his teeth to pull the glove from his right hand. His naked fingers grew numb as they attacked the frozen knot, but he managed to loosen the bindings enough to pull the snowshoe free. He quickly put the glove back on and flexed his fingers to bring warmth back. When the hand felt as if it might work again, he assessed the damage done to the ankle. Any movement of the injured area caused sharp stabs of pain. He would be unable to put any weight on the foot. He was in trouble.

Whitefeather removed his rifle case and brushed the snow from it. He rolled to his hands and knees. He pushed the rifle stock into the snow and used it as leverage to rise, keeping the injured foot in the air. He wobbled awkwardly and almost fell, cursing his stupidity and his throbbing ankle. He roughly beat the snow from his lower body.

Using the rifle as a crutch, Whitefeather hopped on his good foot, like a wounded bird. He sank deep into the snow with every hop, and before long he had no breath to even curse. He stopped often, wheezing, as his leg tightened and threatened to cramp, while his injured ankle sent sharp reminders of its condition. Exhausted and afraid, he forced himself onward. His inner clothes were soaked with sweat, and the chill spread throughout his body.

The taunting wind pummeled him, and when he heard the cry once again, Whitefeather burst into hot tears. Barely able to move by now, and strained to the breaking point, he was almost helpless. He shook as he stood there, wondering if this was to be his death.

With a groan, Whitefeather summoned all his strength and hopped forward. Face contorted with effort, he struggled through the snow. As he thought of the cry, his memory finally brought forth the name of the dread spirit of the north.

Desperate now, reason all but gone, he tumbled into a large drift. Sobbing through a snow-covered face, he tore at the bindings on his remaining snowshoe. His stiff fingers were unable to do the job. Whitefeather clawed for his hunting knife and used it to slash at the bindings. His foot freed, he cast the knife aside. The rifle also lay forgotten in the snow, a victim of his panic.

Rolling to his hands and knees, Whitefeather began to crawl. Instinct alone kept him going to his cabin. He grunted like an animal as his arms and legs sank into the snow. Stripped to the core of his psyche, he formed no more rational thought.

Whitefeather stared dumbly at a tree ahead. It seemed to move, and as it came toward him, the dim outline assumed a more distinct shape. A powerful animal smell assailed Whitefeather's senses, but shattered by his suffering, he could do nothing but watch. A pair of eyes looked back at him. The thing called out, the cry searing through Whitefeather's mind. He screamed once before losing consciousness.

CHAPTER 2

Sue Whitefeather stirred the kettle on the fire and looked at the door. The storm howled around the cabin, and still there was no sign of Jimmy. For the third time, she put her coat and boots on and went outside, quickly pulling the door shut behind her. As the storm swirled around her, she yelled Jimmy's name in the dark. The mocking wind smothered her call, so she followed the age-old method, banging a pot with a metal spoon to guide Jimmy home. She waited, but there was only the wind and the night. She opened the door and slipped back inside, into the light and warmth.

Sue kicked off her boots, hung up her coat, and prepared for the worst. There was no other shelter. If Jimmy didn't return, he could not survive the storm. She refused to cry, for that was not her way.

Life would change, for she could not make it alone out here. She could hunt and trap as well as Jimmy, but it took both of them working together to scratch out a living.

Sue looked at the traps and equipment hung about the interior of the cabin, and sighed. She would sell what she could, but no one would buy the cabin itself. None of the other Crees wanted to live this far out.

Where would she go? Her sister had married; perhaps they would take her in. She shrugged. At least she wouldn't miss Jimmy's temper, or the beatings.

Sue stirred the broth again, and added some herbs. Jimmy might still show up, and if he did, he would be chilled to the bone. Either way, she was ready.

The thump on the door startled her into splashing the broth, almost scalding herself. She ran to the door and hesitated only a moment, afraid in that instant of what might be out there. Then she threw open the door, to the cold and snow pouring into the room over the still form of her husband. She seized his parka and tried to pull him inside. He was much heavier than she, but she was desperate. Grunting with effort, she got him inside and shut the door against the storm.

Sue called his name, and though he didn't respond, she saw he was still breathing. She undressed him where he lay, peeling off the frozen layers of clothing. She grabbed a blanket, spread it on the floor, and rolled Jimmy onto it. Partially covering his nude form, she took a towel and vigorously rubbed his skin. She worked the extremities first, then inward toward the chest. She was relieved to see none of the telltale grayish skin of frostbite, but his flesh was like smooth, polished stone.

By the time she finished, melted snow had formed puddles around his clothes. When she was satisfied that his circulation was good, she gathered two corners of the blanket and hauled him over to the bed.

Sue propped him against the bed, then squatted and used all her strength to hoist him onto it. With his torso on, she lifted his legs and got him up. She dressed him in long underwear and wrapped him in the thick wool blankets. Only then did she stop to catch her breath and rest.

After several minutes, Sue began picking up the discarded clothes. She frowned, noticing that things were missing. Where were Jimmy's snowshoes? How had he managed to get home? His rifle and knife were gone as well, and this worried her even more. Survival out here meant having good equipment, and Jimmy had returned without his. There were no obvious wounds on him.

As the lonely hours ticked by and the fury of the storm abated, Sue kept a close watch on her husband. She rubbed his limbs every half hour, but there was no change. His skin felt like a statue she had once touched in Ottawa. Tomorrow she would have to trek to the Reserve for help. They would send for a doctor, for there was none at the Reserve. Sue stared at the wall, feeling numb. With nothing to do but wait, exhaustion eventually took over, and she dozed.

Sue roused herself when Jimmy stirred and moaned. She went to the pot on the fire, and poured a bowl of the steaming broth. She set the bowl on the rickety table by the bedside.

Sue brushed the hair back from Jimmy's forehead. Feeling heat, she grew curious. His cheeks showed some color now. She turned down the blankets, and felt his chest. His body was heating rapidly, and twitched with a convulsive shudder.

His eyes jerked open, but they were not Jimmy's eyes any longer. Black shiny orbs gazed back at her without any recognition. Jimmy seized her wrist. The movement bumped her against the table, spilling the broth and burning a scream from her. He yanked her closer, and bit deeply into her forearm. She screamed again as blood flowed from her arm, and tried to pull free.

Sue could not break loose from her husband's grip. As her free arm flailed about, she found the overturned bowl. She gripped it and swung it hard against Jimmy's head. He grunted, and struck out at her face. Pain blossomed as her lips split against her teeth. She kept striking him with the bowl, hammering at his head to get free.

Their grim tug-of-war brought him to a standing position. Sue drove her knee into his groin. Air whuffed out of him as he doubled over, but still clinging tenaciously. Dropping the bowl, she raked his face with her nails, tearing bloody furrows. He let go and clubbed her with his arm, knocking her to the floor. Dazed with pain and shock, she tried to scramble away.

Jimmy lunged and caught her ankle. She drew her free leg back and smashed his face with her foot. She kicked again, and his grip loosened. With a mighty effort, she wrenched free and rolled away. She made for the door on unsteady legs, escape the only thing on her mind.

Scrabbling at the latch, she flipped it and threw open the door, and headed out into the night. The thing that had been Jimmy shook his head, stunned by the shock of her ferocious resistance. As he rose to follow, he spied the firewood ax hanging on the wall. With a bloody, torn face, he took the ax and pursued her.

The storm had passed and the night was clear, the moon casting an eerie glow over the grim chase. Sue lunged down the hill through the waist-deep snow, realizing her predicament. Even if she got away from the murderous thing that had been her husband, she had no protection from the cold, and would die before she found shelter. When she turned and saw Jimmy silhouetted in the doorway, she screamed again and frantically clawed her way along.

The thing that had been Jimmy shambled after her, moving in the trail she was breaking. She saw she had no chance of outrunning him in the snow. He would catch her when she collapsed from exhaustion or exposure. Her only chance was to trick him somehow, to get back to the cabin first. The barred door would slow him down enough until she could load one of the other rifles.

Sue began a wide circle to the left. He stayed in her track. Cheeks puffing from the exertion, she kept going by sheer determination. She suddenly cut back up the hill.

Her plan looked like it had worked, for she was closer to the door than he. She concentrated her whole being into moving forward. Her lungs burned as the light beckoned, tantalizingly close.

The ax blade crunched into her right shoulder, knocking her sprawling into the snow. She rolled onto her back, too hurt to even kick out. She watched in horror as he raised the ax overhead. She screamed as it struck with a sickly thud. The ax continued to rise and fall, but there were no more screams. Vapor rose from the mutilated body as crimson splashed the surrounding snow.

Finally, the thing that had been Jimmy Whitefeather threw aside the ax. It seized the body and dragged it back toward the cabin. It had a terrible new hunger.

CHAPTER 3

The waspish buzz of the snowmobile pierced the somber quiet of the forest, harsh and unnatural in the morning air. The man driving the machine went carefully and slowly, towing a toboggan on which his son rode. The man kept looking back to check that all was well, but the boy was grinning, enjoying the ride and holding on tightly.

They were out at the edge of the Reserve, but still on Cree Nation property. They had borrowed the snowmobile and toboggan to get a Christmas tree for the communal building. The man marveled at this new aspect of their lives. He attributed the change to the old priest, who years before had lived with the Crees, and had left many legacies. One of them was an old black-and-white television set, which had made more of a mark than all of his rituals. They only received one channel, but watched in rapt fascination whatever the CBC presented. The little box showed them the world of the whites, the world beyond the forest.

Year by year, the changes crept in. The children had been taken with the idea of Christmas, and resistance eventually broke down. Over strenuous objections about the dying of the past and accepting the ways of the whites, the tribe now allowed a tree to be put up and decorated in the big hall. It had passed by a scant margin in the council.

Snow fell on the man and boy as their passing brushed the branches, a rebuke from the forest for disrupting the silence. They left a twisted track through the trees, searching for just the right one.

The man knew they were close to the Whitefeather cabin. No one from the tribe had seen Jimmy or Sue for some time, but this was not out of the ordinary, since they mostly kept to themselves. On a day like this, though, they might run across Whitefeather running his trapline.

***

What had once been Jimmy Whitefeather lay asleep on the cold cabin floor. The annoying buzzing sound burrowed through the layers of sleep and brought him to consciousness. The noise ground through his head, and he sought the source of irritation. He rose, stumbling over a corpse, and thrashed about the interior of the cabin. He staggered for the door, pawing the latch until it released. He stood oblivious to the inrush of icy air. The sound came again, painful and sharp. He moved down the snowy hill toward the source, to end the noise that hurt.

***

The man heard his son cry out behind him, and braked the machine as he turned around. Pointing, the boy leaped off the toboggan and sank to his waist in the snow. Laughing, he flailed through the white drifts until he stood next to a hardy-looking specimen. The father came up beside him and looked the tree up and down. He walked in solemn silence around it, and finally nodded to the boy, who beamed with pride.

The man walked back to the snowmobile and switched off the engine, leaving the key in. He took out the ax, which had been stowed where it wouldn't move. Holding it just under the blade, he walked back to the tree. He motioned to the boy, who dutifully went to sit on the seat of the snowmobile, out of the way of the swinging ax and flying wood chips.

The man used the ax to knock snow from the branches as he moved around the tree. The snow was not as deep here, and the man cleared more away, for room to chop beneath the lowest branches. He unsnapped and removed the leather sheath from the ax blade. Silently calculating which way he wanted the tree to fall, he took his position and delivered the first blow.

When struck, the tree shuddered as if in pain. The first few strokes bit in at a downward angle. Then the man cut across, making a deep wedge opening in the trunk. Continued hard strokes took out more of the trunk, until the tree gave a sharp crack of protest and toppled over. Two more blows severed it completely from the trunk.

As the man glanced toward his son, he saw a look of surprise, as the boy opened his mouth. Something solid knocked the man down from behind. He rolled onto his back as someone jumped on him, and he brought the ax handle up as a bar against the attacker. As they grappled for leverage on the handle, the father was horrified to recognize a transformed Jimmy Whitefeather, whose features were contorted with rage, and whose matted hair crowned a blood-smeared face. He seemed more beast than human.

Whitefeather snarled and pressed down on the handle. The man yelled at his son to get away, to go for help. The ax handle squeezed against his throat, and he teetered on the edge of consciousness.

The snowmobile engine coughed to life. The sound enraged Whitefeather, who leaped up, tearing the ax from the man's weakened grip. Whitefeather lunged at the source of the sound that so hurt his head, and swung the ax down as the snowmobile lurched away. The blow severed one side of the tow rope, and the toboggan slewed sideways as it was pulled, then flipped free of the other side of the rope. Unable to catch the speeding machine, Whitefeather let out his rage on the toboggan. He smashed the ax with vicious strokes into the wood, and it splintered where it struck.

Whitefeather turned to the man, who was coughing and massaging his injured throat, still trying to breathe. The man never saw the swing of the ax.

CHAPTER 4

Back at the Reserve, the sobbing boy gasped out the story to his people. The horrified crowd turned to Walking Cloud, a respected elder, who took the men to the council house. They quickly made a plan. Eight able-bodied men gathered equipment and set out. Two fast men on cross-country skis went out as scouts, each armed with a rifle, binoculars, and a walkie-talkie. The other six rode in pairs on snowmobiles, one of which was the very one the boy had returned on. They were all armed, and since they did not know what to expect, they carried a first-aid kit and blankets, and two of the snowmobiles each towed a toboggan.

They made their rendezvous at the site where the attack happened, following the earlier track. They looked over the grim scene of smashed toboggan, fallen tree, and gore-stained snow. But the man's body was missing, with a track in the snow showing it had been dragged. The track led in the direction of Whitefeather's cabin. The men exchanged uneasy looks, and followed the track.

The wind was against them as they approached. They stopped at the bottom of the hill leading up to the cabin, and scanned the area with binoculars. A looping, broken track cut through the snow outside the cabin. Most chilling was the patchy red trail going straight to the door.

The silent skiers moved up first, along the side of the hill, with cover from the trees. They aimed their rifles at the cabin door. Another pair stayed at the bottom and trained their guns as well.

On signal, two engines roared to life, bellowing like beasts. They lumbered up the hill at an angle, keeping the lines of fire clear.

The cabin door flew open and something charged out, face and clothing smeared with blood. Through the tangled hair and snarling visage, they recognized Jimmy Whitefeather, and held their fire.

Whitefeather roared a challenge to the metal monsters and made straight for the first one. They drove at him, swerving at the last minute, while the second man on the lead machine caught Whitefeather hard in the chest with a rifle butt as they went by. Whitefeather fell backwards, but rose again to meet the second machine. This pair roared by and the man behind struck Whitefeather in the stomach. He fell to his knees, clutching the injured area. The first pair circled around, and came back for another pass. Whitefeather tried to rise again, but another blow smashed into his back. He fell to his face and lay there.

They cautiously closed in on the outstretched figure. Incredibly, he shook his head and seemed about to rise. He made a feeble swipe before one man knocked him out with a blow to the back of the head. Still wary, they bound him securely and tied him to one of the toboggans that had been brought up. Only then did they approach the cabin.

At first they did not realize what they were looking at, thinking the mess on the floor was an animal carcass. When they understood what lay before them, they were stunned. Three of them went outside and vomited in the snow.

What remained of Sue Whitefeather lay face up by the stove. The fresher corpse of the boy's father occupied the center of the floor, and water around the body showed that the snow on it had barely melted. Whitefeather had already started in. The fearsome wounds gouged by the ax were bad enough, but far worse were the ragged edges of skin torn apart by human teeth.

The shaken men took several minutes to wrap the remains in blankets. They put their grisly bundles on the remaining toboggan, and touched nothing else in this place of horror. There was much evil here, and they wanted no part of it.

The return of the party aroused much curiosity, but the women and children were brusquely sent away. The council met again. They had all heard the boys' tale, and the men now told of what they had found in Whitefeather's cabin. The remains were brought in and viewed.

The shocked silence that followed was broken a single word from the lips of Walking Cloud. It was the name of the ancient, feared enemy, and hovered in the air like a tangible thing. It was the demon spirit of ice and snow, the specter of death that stalked the north woods in the dead of winter. The Wendigo, the demon that made men feast on their fellow humans.

The debate began over what to do with Whitefeather. None spoke of the law of the whites, for this had no bearing on their situation. Walking Cloud spoke of the old tales, and of how Whitefeather's body was now possessed. Having eaten of human flesh, there was no way to save his physical form, but they could set his spirit free. They must drive out the demon of cold, by burning.

The younger men dissented for a time, but the truth could not be denied. They had seen the result of the evil, and could offer up no other way. They had been brought up on these traditions and tales. While belief had faded with age, the evidence lay before them. How else to explain the monstrous horror, but the incarnation of a malevolent spirit?

So in the end, it was agreed. The unconscious body of Whitefeather was taken away, to be guarded for the night. Preparations began for the hideous work of the next day.

Walking Cloud closed his eyes and sought strength for the coming ordeal.

***

Dawn brought a sullen, overcast gloom. Away from the square of Reserve buildings, a pyre had been built. The last bit of night's darkness was leaving the sky when the men entered the clearing. Two of them dragged a bound but struggling Whitefeather between them. There was a path in the piled wood, leading to the tree in the center. The tree was two hands width and had been stripped of all branches. The men propped Whitefeather against the trunk and bound him to it with wire, circling him with coil after coil. When finished, they stepped back through to the outer edge. They pushed the wood in to cover the path, and mounded it up against Whitefeather, until it reached his waist. Taking up two large cans, they doused the whole pile with gasoline.

The men stepped back to join the others who circled the pyre. All of them began to chant in a low, somber tone. Walking Cloud came forth, holding a flaming torch, which flickered madly in the chill morning wind. He spoke in the Cree language, addressing the spirit. He looked Whitefeather directly in the eyes as he set the torch to the pile. The wood erupted in a gush of flame, and sent out a wall of heat so intense that the men had to move farther back. The wood cracked and popped, sending showers of sparks lancing outward.

The air around Whitefeather's head rippled and wavered. As the flames enveloped him, his head whipped from side to side. He writhed in agony, but the wire bound him fast. His hair caught fire, and as it did, his gag came loose. A high, unearthly shriek knifed through the morning air. The screaming and the stench of burning flesh assailed the men and was almost too much to bear. But led by the example of Walking Cloud, they held their ground, and kept up their chanting.

Abruptly, the screaming stopped. The men looked up, but could not see Whitefeather's face for the flames. Walking Cloud nodded, convinced the spirit had left the body, unable to stand the torment of heat. Smoke billowed over the men, watering their eyes and making them cough. Some would later swear that they saw a leering, malevolent face loom up out of the smoke.

The remains of Whitefeather's victims were reverently burned on separate, smaller pyres. It took many hours for all the fires to die down. The fire was good and cleansing. There was one more necessary task, though, so two men were dispatched to burn Whitefeather's cabin to the ground.

Still there was no peace in the hearts of the Crees. Winter had seemed merely long and harsh, but fear now stalked the land, and bore the face of evil.

CHAPTER 5

Sean Laporte stood by the window, looking down at the falling snow. It gently dusted the city of Ottawa with a light, powdery covering. Flakes put sugar-like caps of white on the brightly-colored Christmas decorations, giving the downtown area a fairytale appearance.

He saw the skaters gliding along the frozen Rideau Canal, undaunted by the cold. Children, housewives, even Members of Parliament were out for recreation, or on their way to work, gliding along the canal's length as it wound through the city.

The grey government building in which he worked had no decorations. It loomed over the canal below, and was a solemn monolith that reminded Sean of a prison. The cheerless edifice didn't even have a name on the outside, merely a brass plate with a number. It housed the National Security Bureau, a special branch of the government that received no publicity, and was little-known by the public.

Sean sighed, returned to his desk in the open area, and looked at the report which lay there. He tapped his pen and yawned.

"Are we boring you, Mr. Laporte?"

Sean gulped and recovered. But it was only Billy Chretien. Sean gave his friend an annoyed look. "Jerk. You scared the crap out of me. I thought it was Shepherd."

Billy grinned. "Gotcha. What's the matter? Stay up late watching a hockey game?"

"Actually, I had another nightmare. Couldn't get back to sleep."

The woman at the next desk looked over at Sean and frowned, as if the chitchat was keeping her from important work.

Billy nodded his head in the direction of the water cooler. Sean got up and went to the cooler, pulled down one of the paper cones, and poured a cup of water.

Billy tapped the winking cardboard cutout Santa taped to the plastic jug. "Look at those red cheeks. Looks like Santa's been having some liquid Christmas cheer."

Sean eyed the figure. "Looks more like Pan. Kind of funny, but then again, Christmas was originally a pagan holiday."

"How come you know all that mythology stuff?"

"Took some courses at University, while I was getting my Criminal Justice degree."

Billy grunted. "You as bored as I am?"

"If these windows weren't sealed, I'd jump out of one."

"Only two days to Christmas. We gotta hang in that long."

"I know, I'm just restless," Sean sighed. "I'm not playing in my hockey league this season, and that usually calms me down."

Billy smiled. "Yup, nothing like bashing a few guys against the boards to get you in the Christmas spirit."

"Not much of that this year, I'm afraid."

"How come?"

"Ah, I don't know."

Billy looked concerned. "You and Ree getting along okay?"

"Yeah, yeah, that's not it, everything's fine. It's just..."

"What?"

Sean crushed his empty cup and dropped it in the wastebasket. "That nightmare last night spooked me. Guess I'm feeling a little stale. I'm thirty-two and still pushing papers behind a desk. And I'm going to be getting married and settling down and all, and Ree wants a ton of kids. Sometimes I feel like, shit, this is it. This is the rest of my life."

Billy looked serious, unusual for him. "Well, that's pretty fucking depressing."

"Tell me about it. I mean, listen."

The two of them looked out at the other desks. Sean went on. "It's like a morgue in here. So many people out for the holidays, and the ones left are all wrapped up in their own thoughts, like Christmas gifts. It's too damn quiet."

Billy nodded. "Okay. Watch this." He opened the drawer of a nearby file cabinet and slammed it shut with a bang. Six heads bobbed up and six pairs of eyes skewered the transgressor. Billy shrugged and gave his best apologetic smile. In unison, the heads bobbed back down to their work.

"Did you see that? It's like a flock of those drinking-glass novelty birds."

The image made Sean chuckle.

Billy beamed, but immediately changed his expression to serious. "Uh-oh, here comes Peggy, and she's got that look." She stood before them.

"He did it," said Billy, pointing to Sean.

"Mr. Shepherd would like to see you both in his office." She turned and left. Sean and Billy looked at each other.

"What'd we do now?"

Sean smiled. "He probably figured out that you gave him that whoopie cushion for a Secret Santa gift last year."

"Nah, probably wants to give us a big bonus for Christmas."

"The game's afoot, Watson," said Sean. "Let's go see what kind of trouble we're in."

When confronted by the solid door with the tasteful nameplate, Sean felt like a recalcitrant schoolboy called before the Headmaster. He shrugged, and gave a cursory knock as he turned the handle and entered, Billy on his heels.

Gordon Shepherd stood looking out the window, with his back to the room. His office was Spartan austerity, conspicuously neat and orderly, like the man himself. A single framed photograph of his wife was the only adornment. Having no children, he put his all into running the department with a firm hand and an efficient, no-nonsense attitude.

Sean, who always looked a bit weathered, wondered how Shepherd always looked so crisp and fresh-pressed. Everyone referred to him out of his hearing as "The Good Shepherd" who ran "his flock." It was a measure of how successful he was that he had survived all the political battles that occurred every time the government changed parties.

"Please have a seat," Shepherd said. He hadn't turned around.

Sean and Billy exchanged glances. Easing into one of the chairs in front of the massive desk, Sean noticed a large relief map of Ontario Province pinned to the wall. He said nothing, knowing Shepherd would speak in his own time. Though outwardly calm, Sean's pulse quickened, sensing something important.

Shepherd finally turned to face them. Sean was surprised to see Shepherd's face lined with concern, as he normally maintained a strict poker face.

"We have a problem on our hands," Shepherd began. "It could become much bigger, and very nasty, unless we handle it with the utmost care and discretion."

Sean and Billy kept silent and watched Shepherd walk over to the map before he spoke again.

"Strung across northern Ontario up towards Hudson's Bay is a series of government Reserves for the various native peoples of the region. A small tribe of Crees lives on this one here, in an otherwise sparsely populated, desolate region.

There's little in the way of mining, industry, or even timber, and most sportsmen go elsewhere.

"A few days ago, unusual trouble erupted. A member of the tribe murdered his wife and another man in separate incidents. When captured, it was discovered that he had cannibalized the bodies. They didn't turn him over to the authorities, but took matters into their own hands and burned the man at the stake."

"Christ," said Billy.

"That's not all," Shepherd went on. "Apparently these Crees have a legend about some spirit that induces a state of cannibalism. These people claim that the man they burned had fallen under the spell."

"In this day and age?" Sean replied, shaking his head.

"Indeed. We're sending you two up there to find out the facts. To determine just what happened, and whether this spirit thing is a smokescreen of some sort. Although I'm sure if they wanted to kill someone and get away with it, they could have come up with something a bit more plausible."

"Background on this spirit thing?" Sean said. He flipped open a small notebook and clicked a pen.

"There's a book about it, written by a Doctor Atherton, who teaches at McGill. Since this angle seems important, we thought you should speak with him. He's helped local authorities on other matters before this, and is thought to be confidential and reliable. He's at home in Montreal, and he agreed to meet with you tomorrow to discuss it.

"This thing is called a 'Wendigo'." Shepherd spelled it out as Sean wrote the name at the top of a page.

Shepherd pointed back to the map. "We would prefer you both to get up there as quickly as possible, but right now they're having a storm that won't clear until late Christmas Day. The area is fairly inaccessible, so we'll have you fly to Thunder Bay and have you take a helicopter out to the site. At least you both get to spend Christmas at home."

"Thank you, sir," said Sean. "Ree will be happy to hear that."

Shepherd stopped a moment and put an approximation of a smile on his face. "How is Miss Tourneau?"

"She's fine, thank you. Making her plans for the wedding."

"You can tell her she won't have to miss you for long. We'd like a quick resolution to this thing. If the wire services get hold of this story, they'll turn it into a ghoulish journalistic circus. So you'll report only to me."

Billy spoke. "How did we hear about this in the first place?"

"A rare stroke of luck. There's a retired Royal Canadian Mounted Police officer who lives up there and acts as a part-time government liaison. He's worked with the Crees before, and they apparently trust him as much as they do any outsider. He realized the explosive nature of this situation, and called someone over on Parliament Hill, who then called us.

"The man's name is Peter Carroway. Stellar record, and word is he's very reliable. There are no facilities up there, so you'll both stay with him. You may be roughing it. He'll provide you with transportation, and assist you in whatever you need."

"All right," said Sean as he finished his notes. "What about this Atherton?"

"He's expecting you tomorrow morning. Don't get into particulars. Here's his address, and you can go straight there tomorrow without stopping here. Just call to check in and see if there are any developments.

"You'll need your French up there," Shepherd went on. "They speak their own tongue, of course, and some English, but you'll do better in French, from what we hear. Dress warmly, and good luck."

"Thank you for having confidence in us, sir," said Sean. "We'll do our best."

They left the office, and Billy whistled low. "Son of a bitch. Cannibals for Christmas. Good thing I got you barbecue sauce for a gift."

"Very funny. Shall I pick you up in the morning?"

"How come I never get to drive?" Billy pouted.

"Because you're a maniac."

"You say that like it's a bad thing. They all drive like maniacs in Montreal, you know."

"Yeah, but I want to get there and back in one piece."

"What's Ree going to say about this?"

Sean sighed. "She's going to be pissed."

CHAPTER 6

When Sean got back to the apartment, Ree wasn't home from work yet. He frowned, because she almost always made it home before him, and now that he had big news, he was eager to share it.

He opened a cold bottle of Molson's and sipped it while he searched for a map of Montreal. He found one in a drawer under a pile of papers, and pulled out his notes for Atherton's Montreal address. He located the street on the map, and planned his route. He went to the bedroom and tossed the map onto the bed so he wouldn't forget it.

He heard Ree come in, and went to greet her with an embrace and a kiss.

"Mmmm," she responded, then sniffing, made a face. "Ugh, beer breath." Moving away, she took off her coat and hung it up, and removed her boots.

Though he was almost jittery with the desire to tell, he knew it was better to let her get settled in before springing it. "How'd work go?"

"Same old stuff. But it's holiday time, so here I am, an independent career woman, university-educated, capable, and I'm baking cookies for the office Christmas party."

"What's so bad about that?"

"I'll bet *you* never baked cookies for *your* office."

Sean grinned. "I work for the government. They don't allow us menfolk to do that sort of thing."

"Chauvinists," she snorted. "Speaking of which, I'm going to change and make dinner."

"You're a little late tonight."

Ree stared at him, blushing. "What?"

"Did you stop off somewhere?"

"Oh." She laughed, a harsh sound, like rain battering a tin can. "I, uh, had to make a stop. Christmas shopping."

"You've always been a bad liar. Someone's got a secret."

Ree swallowed, and then abruptly turned away. When she spoke, her voice was too casual. "You okay with chicken for dinner?"

"Sure." Sean frowned. Damn it, he wanted to tell her, but now he knew there was something she needed to say. He followed her into the bedroom.

She held up the map he had left out. "What's this for?"

Sean sat on the bed. "I wanted to tell you. I finally got a field assignment."

Ree stiffened. "But you've always been at the office."

"I know, but with so many people out for the holidays, they're short-handed on field ops."

"What kind of field assignment?"

"A murder."

Ree let out a sound.

"What's wrong?"

She burst into tears.

"What the hell, Ree?"

"*Now*? After all this time, *now* they put you in danger?"

"What do you mean? You know they can send me out at any time. Are you worried about Christmas?"

"No. I'm not worried about *Christmas*."

"Then what?"

"I went to the doctor today. That's why I was late."

Sean froze, waiting for the blow. Some terminal disease? Is that why she was crying?

"I'm pregnant."

Sean's thoughts did a complete backflip.

Ree looked at him. "Say something."

"I— that's great. Jesus, I thought you were going to tell me you had cancer or something." Then he whooped and went to hug her.

She was still crying. "But everything's ruined now."

"What do you mean?"

"My family. It's bad enough for them that we're living together and not married, and now this."

"Well, they're just going to have to get over it. We told them we couldn't afford two separate apartments. Goddamnit, we're going to be married in a few months. If that's not good enough for them, too bad."

"Don't say that."

"What am I supposed to say? We're going to have a baby. This is the greatest news, and all you can talk about is what they're going to think. Aren't you happy?"

"Of course I'm happy."

"So why are you still crying?"

"The wedding."

"What about it?"

She had a tissue out, and was dabbing at her eyes. "We'll have to move it up. January."

"Why?"

"You think they could all sit there in that church while I waddle down the aisle in my white wedding dress, looking like a pregnant hippo?"

Sean looked at her. "Screw 'em. We'll elope."

"You know we can't do that."

"We can do any damned thing we want. It's our wedding."

"They're my family."

"I'm your family too," Sean tried to keep the irritation out of his voice. "I want what's best for you, not for them."

"They're just a bit old-fashioned."

"If it makes you unhappy, then maybe they should get over their nineteenth-century views and join the modern world."

"Don't talk about them like that."

"So we'll get married in January. We can tell them when we go over for Christmas."

"No."

"What?"

"We can't tell them. We can't ruin Christmas for them."

"Ruin it," Sean shook his head. "Anybody else would be happy for you."

"You've got to promise me you won't say anything. We'll tell them after the holidays."

"Fine. Whatever."

"Don't be that way."

"The second happiest day of my life, and I'm supposed to worry about the attitudes of a bunch of old people who think you're a loose woman living in sin."

"I am."

Sean grinned. "And I love you for it."

Ree cracked a smile. "I know." Then her frown returned. "But you said they put you on a murder."

"Yeah." Sean refocused his thoughts. "Billy and I are driving to Montreal tomorrow to talk to a professor, but we'll be back for dinner. Then the day after Christmas, we fly up to Thunder Bay and into the backcountry. Shouldn't be away too long."

"How damned decent of them to let you have Christmas off."

"Thank the weather up there more than anything. They had their way, we'd be up there now. This is something that could cause a lot of bad publicity."

"Is it dangerous?"

Sean shrugged. "Just a delicate situation we have to keep out of the press."

"Can you tell them to send someone else?"

Sean looked at her. "It's my first big case, my first chance to get out in the field."

She looked like the tears might return. "You're excited to be going."

"Hell yes. I've been stuck in that damn office for too long. I need this."

"I need *you.*"

"It's just a few days. This could give me the real boost I've been looking for. Most of the time the worst I have to worry about is a nasty paper cut." Sean smiled.

"Is that why you've been so moody lately?"

"I guess so. I'm in a rut. I haven't been working out, haven't been playing hockey. The last time we went skiing, I ached for three days. I'm getting out of shape just sitting around. I have to get out, get moving a little."

"But a murder..."

"I'll have Billy with me."

"Is that supposed to make me feel better?"

"What do you have against him?"

"Nothing. But I need you to stay safe."

"I will. I promise."

Sean decided to keep the details about cannibalism to himself.

CHAPTER 7

"Look out!" yelled Billy.

Sean hit the brakes, missing by bare centimeters the Mercedes that had sliced in front of them. The heavy holiday traffic of Montreal was a brutal battle of nerves, with impatient drivers suddenly darting into any open space between vehicles.

"Can I shoot him?" Billy asked.

"No."

"You never let me have any fun."

"Just stay on lookout for me. That one was close."

The traffic had slowed down to a crawl again, and they watched the line of cars.

"This is Christmas," Billy said. "People should be happy. But everyone looks so frustrated."

"There has to be a better way of getting from one place to another," said Sean.

"Too damn many people."

"When rats are put into overcrowding situations, they get violent and berserk. I think people get the same way."

"There's a Volkswagen," said Billy. "It does look like a giant beetle, doesn't it? Don't all these cars remind you of insects? The outsides are kind of like an insect shell, a whaddyacallit?"

"A carapace," offered Sean.

"Yeah, that's it. They're like stink-beetles, spewing noxious gases. A whole army of stink-beetles."

Sean glanced over. "What goes on in that head of yours?"

"Just trying to pass the time. You get to drive. I'm bored."

"Play the radio, then."

"Nothing but damned Christmas music on. If I hear 'Silent Frigging Night' one more time, I'm gonna scream."

"Well, let's not then. We'll play a game. I spy, with my eye, something that begins with 'c'."

Billy looked at him suspiciously. "Car?"

"Oh, damn, you got it." Sean grinned.

Billy theatrically huffed and turned away, arms crossed over his chest.

They inched into Montreal.

"If you're not too busy, could you get the map and tell me where to get off for Sherbrooke Street?"

"I'll tell you where to get off," Billy muttered.

"Be good, or I'll tell Santa."

"Fine." There was a rustling of map before Billy looked up at road signs, and another map consultation. "Next exit."

"See, that wasn't so hard."

Billy harrumphed and put the map away. He sulked for a bit until they got into the downtown, and then became animated at seeing the bustle. "Look at that babe. Hey, are we gonna get out while we're here? The clubs are more fun than in Ottawa."

Sean shot Billy a quick glance. "I'll drop you off before I head back."

"Just because you're getting married and can't have fun anymore doesn't mean I have to suffer."

"Yes it does. Ah. There's McGill," Sean said as they drove past. "Looks nice, all frosted with clean snow."

Billy rattled off the street names. "Turn here."

Sean turned, and Billy had him turn again down a side street.

"Now this is the neighborhood for a professor," said Billy. "Tree-lined, residential, quiet, older places. I want one like this someday."

"With what you spend on beer, if you quit drinking, you'd probably be able to save enough."

"Yeah, but what's life without beer?"

"We want number twenty-seven," said Sean.

"There's sixteen. Other side."

"There it is. Where the hell can I park? Nothing but snowbanks everywhere."

"Yeah, don't they have snow removal? Park in the driveway there."

They got out and stretched, unknotting their muscles after the cramping car ride.

A thin, slightly stooped man of medium height opened the front door when they knocked. He wore an unbuttoned cardigan sweater over a flannel shirt, with loose fitting slacks and slippers. From the gray, receding hair and black-framed glasses, Sean guessed him to be in his early sixties.

"Doctor Atherton? I'm Sean Laporte, from Ottawa. This is Billy Chretien."

"Yes, come right in," Atherton said, taking the proffered hands for a polite shake. He closed the door after they had come in, and took their coats. He looked down at their winter boots and frowned.

"Would you mind very much taking those off? The floors, you know."

Sean and Billy removed their boots and followed Atherton down a hallway. The sensation of padding along in his stocking feet reminded Sean of when he was a kid in his aunt's house. The feeling intensified when he had to ask permission to use the bathroom.

The little room was plain, lacking feminine touches. Sean saw a framed print of a Hieronymus Bosch painting on the wall, and instantly knew that Atherton lived alone. Only a single man would put up something like that in a bathroom. It also told him that Atherton was a bit out of the common herd.

When Sean came out, he was shown to the study, with a huge, cluttered desk and overstuffed bookcases.

"Thank you for taking the time to see us," Sean said.

"Not at all," Atherton replied. "Can I offer you something to drink? I was just putting on some tea."

"That would be nice, thank you." Sean looked at Billy, who nodded.

Atherton left to put the kettle on, and Billy instantly bounded up to scan the piles of books on the desk, the floor, and the shelves.

"Man, I've never seen so many books. Look at them. These ones are in French, and that pile has titles in German. Guy's got his own fortress of learning."

"Sit down before he comes back. He'll think you're snooping."

"I *am* snooping." Billy sat anyway.

Atherton came back and tried to clear books from his desk. He moved stacks from one place to another, and in vain looked around for empty spaces on which to put them. He eventually gave up and set three piles on the floor.

"That's better, now I can see you. Writing another book, I'm afraid. But you're interested in only one of mine, isn't that right? '*Legends of the Northern Indigenous People*'? Have you read it?"

"I'm afraid not," confessed Sean. "We just heard about it yesterday."

"Well, you have missed a treat," said Atherton smiling. "I enjoyed that one. A little something more than those tedious academic endeavors that are nothing more than pretexts to help us old professors keep our jobs. That's one of my better sellers. In fact, it was nominated for a Governor General's Award."

Atherton searched a shelf behind him and pulled out a book. "Here, take a copy. My Christmas gift to the government. On second thought, maybe I'll bill them." Atherton smiled to show he was joking. "Why is the government interested in the Wendigo?"

"We heard it's some kind of cannibal spirit," Sean said. "Can you tell us about that?"

"Yes. It is the physical representation of hunger in an environment where starvation is a constant danger in the winter," said Atherton. "It is the greatest misfortune to encounter it, for as legend goes, if it doesn't kill you, it turns you into a monster with the craving for human flesh."

"Something like a werewolf, or a vampire then," Billy said with a grin. Atherton frowned. A high-pitched whistling came from the other room, and he went to attend to it.

Sean opened the book he had been given and flipped through it. He found a black-and-white illustration of a horrible, wild-eyed demon devouring a man, and showed it to Billy. The demon was large, about twice the size of the man, and the detail in the picture was gruesome. Atherton came back with a tray of tea things, and saw what Sean was looking at. Sean closed the book.

Atherton set the tray on the space he had made on the desk, and prepared the cups. He carefully poured the first and handed it to Sean, who noted the delicate bone china. Ree would probably know what brand it was, Sean thought, and handled the cup with care, worried that he might damage it. He saw Billy take a cup with something akin to fear in his eyes. Sean shook his head. He preferred things that were more practical and sturdy for everyday use.

"You were looking at the illustration," Atherton said. "Rather like Goya's picture of Saturn devouring his children." He chuckled as he took his own cup in hand, and sipped. "We get away with Grand Guignol when we can. As you can tell from the print in the bathroom, I enjoy a touch of the macabre now and then. Necessary, I suppose, when one deals with the cannibal aspect.

"I suppose we should start at the beginning." He set down the cup and steepled his fingers together. Sean noted the melodramatic gesture, but said nothing. The professor probably enjoyed lecturing people.

"Legends of the Wendigo go back hundreds of years, old before the Europeans came to the continent. French and English explorers heard the tales from many tribes they encountered, all over the central and eastern provinces, and down in the States as well. There are an astonishing number of geographical features named for this spirit, especially rivers and lakes. There are spelling variants, but the essential idea remains the same."

Atherton sipped his tea. "The tribes where the belief is strongest are the Cree, Ojibwa, and Algonquin. There are many differences, but it is generally known as a shapeshifter, and can even take the form of a man. It can be small, but is more often the size of a giant. It can be fur or flesh, or ice and snow."

"Frosty, the Abominable Snowman?" Billy laughed.

Atherton set down his cup so that it rattled. "Are you taking this seriously?"

"What?"

"I cannot believe you are wasting my time, making jokes about this."

"Sorry, professor. I stopped believing in monsters long ago."

"Don't patronize me, young man. I've devoted many years to the study of Native People lore, and I do not need you to come here and mock their long-held beliefs."

Sean set down his own cup. "I'm sure he didn't mean to make fun of you or your work, sir. We just find this fantastic that we're dealing with a case involving a belief in some fairy-tale creature that goes around eating people. If either his or my reaction was inappropriate, I apologize."

Atherton leaned forward. "You mean there's been a report of a Wendigo incident? That's what this is about?"

Sean realized he'd said too much in trying to smooth things over. "You know we can't share details of an active investigation. We're just looking for background."

"But you can confirm there's an actual incident where someone referenced the Wendigo?"

"Maybe they're going for an insanity defense," Billy said.

Atherton looked at them over his glasses. "Are either of you Catholic?"

"Yes," they replied.

"Do you believe in the tenets of your religion?"

"Of course."

"So you believe in a great many fantastical things that have happened throughout history, as every saint of your church has miracles attached to their name."

"That's different," Sean objected.

"Of course. *Your* belief in supernatural phenomena is perfectly rational and acceptable, while someone else's is the quaint superstition of a savage."

Sean had no response. He refused to look over at Billy.

Atherton went on. "Don't you understand what all this is about? These beliefs are the stories a people make up to explain their place in the world. The tales and parables are to illustrate ideas about those beliefs. Let's take, for example, the story of David and Goliath. What would you say that represents?"

"That with belief in God, you can overcome anything, even against impossible odds."

"That's right. Here are a people constantly at war, surrounded by enemies, overpowering enemies. So one of the important central stories, core beliefs, is of this puny, powerless shepherd boy defeating a superior juggernaut of a warrior, where no one else could. Now their enemy is not so fearsome and invulnerable.

"There are also numerous David-and-Goliath stories in Wendigo lore, showing that heroes can sometimes defeat this powerful monster. This Wendigo is a demon, and demons are a basic belief in church lore as well. One must show the opposition as incredibly strong to prove one's superiority."

"But—"

"And with every demon, every possessing spirit, you must have a way to defeat it, to exorcise it. Even your church still has rituals for that. Magic incantations, special objects, that sort of thing. What is a priest but a type of shaman, a man who is a special mystical conduit to the unseen world?"

Sean sat back.

Billy jumped in. "So how do you beat a Wendigo?"

"You can't match its strength, so you outsmart it. Use your proverbial sling, as David did. Use a weapon it has not encountered, and therefore is not expecting. To exorcise the demon, which is of ice and snow, use the opposite, which is heat, to drive the demon from the flesh.

"Winters in the north woods tend to extreme conditions. Food is scarce, hunger rampant. Isolation and starvation preying on the mind. Picture a small group of people, bound together, cut off from the world for long, cold months. The wind howling outside, the food gone, and only one way to survive. By nourishing yourself on a friend or family member. Some people give in to the ultimate taboo, and feed on their fellow man.

"So it is 'explained away' by the appearance of a 'spirit.' When discovered, the afflicted person is dealt with, using harsh measures. The guilty are punished, life goes on.

"Some chose to die rather than go that route. But others succumbed. In our hemisphere, it's rather rare, but not completely unknown. It is a taboo rarer than the most extreme forms of incest. It removes the last vestige of civilization, puts the person on the level of the animals, and makes the practitioner the ultimate outcast. You're familiar with our own Martin Hartwell story, and the tale of the soccer players in the Andes after their plane crashed?"

Sean nodded.

"How to explain such a thing? Makes one a bit nervous, with ten feet of snow outside the cabin and the last of the food being divided up.

"So voila, the monster is not within us, but is an external force. Just stay away from the bogeyman, and all will be well."

"So the idea of this thing was born as an explanation for horrible acts?" Sean said. "To cover their fears?"

"Man has always been a frightened, superstitious creature. Our superior brains also let us know how dreadfully alone we are in the cosmos. Our greatest fear is of being by ourselves in an empty universe, on the darkling plane of time and space. So we invent company. We fill the universe with beings that create and run things. Better to have capricious gods than nothingness. We invent all-powerful overseers, and shift the blame for our actions and tragedies onto outside agencies. Everyone did it, from Egyptians, Assyrians, Greeks, Polynesians, Chinese, to natives in the Americas. All had their pantheon of immortal, omnipotent beings with fickle natures, which accounts for ill fortune and catastrophe: floods, earthquakes, volcanoes, crop failures, and invasions. Propitiate and petition the gods correctly, and maybe they'll keep the calamity away. Better that, than to think of an indifferent, chaotic universe with no reason and no protection whatsoever.

"Furthermore, there are often sides drawn up, one set of gods that helps Man, by opposing the ones who seek to destroy him. There are hierarchies, and the Wendigo is one of the 'bad guys,' a lower-order demon. But what it really represents is a dark corner of the human existence, a scapegoat born of a complex guilt system, a spirit created by a need."

"Pretty powerful image," Sean said.

"Indeed. It fires the imagination. Algernon Blackwood wrote a classic Wendigo story. A singer named Mary McCaslin has a haunting song about it. Here, let me play it for you."

Atherton slipped a tape into a machine and pressed the Play button. Sean closed his eyes and listened. There was a low, instrumental moaning counterpoint to the voice of the singer, a rumbling undercurrent that suggested menace. Violins wailed eerily, and the high, clear song left a haunting residue, the words evoking dread and awe.

Sean opened his eyes, impressed. He looked over at Billy, who raised his eyebrows. Atherton nodded.

"Yes, it perfectly captures the feeling, don't you think?"

"It certainly does."

"What else can I tell you about it?"

"You've given us a good background. Billy, do you have any more questions?" Billy shook his head.

As he got up, Sean heard a floorboard creak above them. He looked sharply at Atherton. "Is there someone else in the house?"

Atherton turned pale. "I live alone."

"No housekeeper, guest? It sounded like someone was above us."

"We're quite alone, I assure you."

"We contacted you with the assurance of confidentiality."

"I'm quite aware of my responsibilities. I resent your accusations."

"I heard something."

"It's an old house."

"I suppose so."

"Let me show you out."

They walked back to the doorway, and Sean and Billy put on their coats and boots. They all stood in awkward silence for a moment.

"Well, thank you, Professor. Merry Christmas."

"Oh. Yes. Merry Christmas to you. And good luck in your research."

Back in the car, Billy laughed until he coughed. "Jesus, what a load."

"What?"

"All that psych mumbo-jumbo. Man, if I ever kill someone, I'll just chaw on them a little and call this guy in as an expert witness to tell them I'm crazy."

"There's something else," Sean said.

"What's that?"

"He lied to us. There was definitely someone else in the house. I saw a curtain twitch upstairs when we left."

"Why would he do that?"

"Don't know," said Sean. "A reporter, maybe? If so, he's in a lot of trouble. But now I need you to act normal, and sneak a look in your side mirror."

Billy chattered and waved his hands as if telling a story. "Black Saab? About three cars back?"

"That's the one. Pulled out after us when we left Atherton's."

"Want to lose them?"

"Hell, no. I want to find out who it is."

Sean slowed and looked back, but the Saab passed them on the left, streaking ahead. "Did you see him?"

"Sure did," said Billy. "I didn't know gorillas could drive. Especially ones that big. And the plate was dirty, couldn't get the number."

"Maybe he wasn't following us after all."

"Or maybe he figured you'd made him. Say, you don't think he bugged the car, do you?"

Sean glanced at Billy. "Shit. I'm pulling over. Get that blanket out of the trunk. I'm going to have a look."

Twenty minutes later, Sean was trying to warm himself from the car's heater vent. Billy got back in.

"Nothing. You?"

"Nothing," Sean tried to keep his teeth from chattering. "We'll have them check it back in Ottawa, just to be sure."

"Are we getting paranoid? You sure that guy was tailing us?"

"I'm not sure of anything anymore."

"Should we be carrying our service weapons?"

"Like I'd trust you with a gun," Sean smiled.

CHAPTER 8

The annoying buzz of the alarm clock cut off when Sean slammed the button. He groaned, burying his face in the pillow. Ree sat up and stretched, rubbed her eyes, and gently poked him in the ribs. "Morning, you. Merry Christmas."

She got a muffled reply. She kissed his shoulder and the back of his neck. Sean rolled up to kiss her. Then he burrowed back down.

Ree poked him again. "Come on, get up. We have to get to Mass."

"Later."

"We can't. We have to be at my parents'."

Sean groaned again.

"Don't be like that."

"Bad enough to get up early on Christmas Day," Sean opened one eye to look at her. "Then I have to go be nice to all those cousins, aunts, and uncles. Can't keep them all straight. There's too many of them. And they tell stories about people I don't know. Then they ask me about my work, and I can't talk about it, and they look at me like I'm crazy. Then there's your cousin, the Quebecois separatist, who thinks I'm only there to spy on him."

"You're part of that family now. So get up."

"Can't we skip Mass, just this once?"

"Sean!"

"All right, you don't have to yell. I know, I'm evil for even thinking it."

"I though you liked Mass."

"Where'd you get that idea? You're the one who enjoys it. It's kind of like a play where they're going through the motions."

"I hope you're not losing your faith."

Ree got up and slipped into a robe to go shower. Sean watched her and wondered why she had to put something on to go a few steps and take it off again. It was just one of those things women did that he could never understand.

When they were in church a short time later, Sean kept fidgeting as he worked hard to stifle his yawns. Perhaps he hadn't got immersed in the religion early enough, he thought. He looked around at the children in the pews, wondering what they would believe when they grew up. Probably just what their parents believed. He wondered if his children would get Ree's faith, or his relentless questioning of the comfortable platitudes. His children. Ree's news put Sean in awe of the thought of having a family, as he hadn't the faintest notion of how to raise kids.

The service droned on, and Sean daydreamed. He got through somehow, and later, in the car on the way to Ree's parents, they passed an elaborate Nativity scene, and Sean stared at it in wonder. It seemed so stark and primitive.

Ree was driving, humming 'Joy to the World.' She glanced over. "You're not very merry this Christmas."

"Steeling myself for the ordeal."

"Come on. They're not that bad."

"Just overwhelming. So many of them. I'm not used to the noise level in rooms that size."

She reached over and squeezed his arm. "Was it tough, being an only child?"

"Not when my parents were alive."

"I can't imagine not being with family."

"That's one reason you like church so much. It's an extension. But I always feel like the outsider."

"You sound like David Copperfield."

"How about Tiny Tim? 'God Bless Us, every one.'"

"Here we are. It looks so pretty with all the decorations." Ree parked the car. "Remember, not a word about the baby. We'll tell them after the holidays, when we've made plans."

When they got out, Sean saw a black Lincoln Town Car cruise by the street in front of the house. He frowned, realizing he had seen one when he came out of the church. A sliver of cold went down the back of his neck. Was he being followed?

Sean and Ree loaded up with presents and went to ring the doorbell. They were engulfed by hugging people as soon as they walked in. Their coats and gifts were whisked away, and they endured handshakes, kisses, and a barrage of questions.

Sean only got a break because someone else arrived, and the sequence was repeated with the newcomers. He escaped to the kitchen and got a beer, before joining the men in the living room. He found an unoccupied chair and sat, grateful for the respite.

This was Sean's second Christmas with the Tourneau clan. As such, he was not under heavy pressure to make constant conversation, nor was he excluded from the discussion, a relentless babble in French and English.

With a sense of wonder, he watched the interactions. The men laughed and joked, while the women stayed in the kitchen and dining room, preparing the meal. The adolescents, caught in their netherworld age between children and adults, sulked or remained aloof. Children ran through the place in a frenzy, enduring scoldings when they got too rambunctious. They kept getting shooed away from the lavishly decorated Christmas tree, piled high with a mountain of gifts.

Sean stared moodily at the tree, slipping away, until it seemed to shimmer and change. The brightly-wrapped gifts turned dull and brown, looking like pieces of wood. The treetop angel descended and lost its wings and halo, becoming a man. The blinking tree lights spouted flame, which caught the branches and spread. The angel-man was tied to the tree, and the flames enveloped him. He appeared to scream, but no sound came out.

Sean shuddered and rubbed his eyes with thumb and forefinger. He was startled to realize that someone was speaking to him. He stood on unsteady legs, mumbled an excuse, and slipped away.

He moved through the throng as if in a dream. He found himself in the kitchen, blinking in surprise. Ree was at the stove, stirring something in a pot, and talking with a large woman who wore shiny silver earrings that reminded Sean of fishing lures. Ree saw him from the corner of her eye and smiled. She spoke to the woman and gave her the spoon. She glided over to Sean and slipped an arm around his waist, giving him a squeeze as she planted a kiss on his cheek.

Like the princess kissing the frog, the spell was broken. He was brought back from the mists in an instant, his mind once again alert and clear. He looked at his anchor to reality and realized how much he loved her.

Somehow he made it through the opening of the presents and the huge meal, where he ate two plates of food, and was urged to eat still more.

After the meal wound down, people went out to the living room to tell favorite old family stories. Sean hated this part, because he had either heard them or didn't know or care about the rest. He grew bored and restless when they were ribbing each other and making inside jokes. He felt hollow, and he could feel a dull headache beginning.

Ree finally came and took his hand so they could begin making their goodbyes. It took a good half-hour after that before they were done and out the door.

In the car on the way home, he stared out the window.

"Did you have to get drunk?" Ree's voice was sharp.

"What are you talking about? I'm not drunk."

"People were telling me you were staggering around the living room and slurring your words."

"They should mind their own goddamned business. I got up and my knee went out from under me, that's all. I had one beer. Sorry I wasn't the life of the party."

"I wish you'd make a little more effort to be sociable." Ree went on talking, but Sean was looking in the mirror at the headlights of the car behind them.

"Pull over."

"Are you going to be sick?"

"What? No. Pull the damn car over."

Ree braked and swerved the car to the curb. Sean watched a long dark car pass them. A Lincoln, he was sure of it. The same one.

"What is it?"

If he told her they were being followed, she'd cause a fuss and be worried. "I saw them weaving, like the driver was drunk. Didn't want them hitting us."

"Honestly, sometimes I don't know what gets into you."

CHAPTER 9

An irritating buzz pulled Sean from his dream, and he groped for the alarm clock. He had been a cowboy on a covered wagon, fighting giant, shadowy Indians. Sitting up, he rubbed a hand over his face and through his hair. He came to his senses slowly, pieces of the dream still lingering.

Sean shambled off to the bathroom. He stayed longer than usual in the shower, savoring the hot spray, knowing he would be gone from the comforts of home for several days.

Ree came in, smiling and sleepy-eyed. She hugged him from behind, head pressed into his broad back. He turned and hugged her in return. Conscious of his imminent departure, they were silent and reflective as they ate their breakfast. Sean finished and went to dress.

Ree joined him in the bedroom as he packed. She said nothing until he took out the holster that held his service pistol.

"I hate when you have to carry that thing."

Sean embraced her. "Don't worry, I've never had to use it. I only take it because I'm supposed to."

"Why is it you men run off to do stupid, dangerous things, while we women stay behind and get to wonder if we'll ever see you again?"

Sean finished packing, while Ree's eyes stung from the tears she held back.

Ree drove Sean to Billy's apartment, threading her way through the traffic. She took her eyes from the road long enough to look at Sean, and he smiled back reassuringly. He felt guilty about being so happy to leave. He thought that a few days away from the desk and the paperwork would be just fine, even if his mission was a bit macabre.

Billy met them at the curb outside, opened the back, tossed in his bag, and scooted inside the car. They continued on to the airport.

Sean turned back to speak to Billy, and saw a black Lincoln behind them.

"You okay, man?" Billy was speaking. "You look like you've seen a ghost."

Sean mumbled an excuse. He wasn't about to worry Ree while he got on a plane to leave town. But he kept stealing glances in the side mirror. The car stayed with them, a few vehicles back.

Ree parked in front of the terminal, and Sean and Billy took out their bags. Sean watched a tall man get out of the Lincoln, which had pulled to the curb behind them.

Ree stepped out of the car to hug Sean. "You better come back." She tried to sound tough, but her voice was thick, and her eyes were wet.

"Count on it," he said, and kissed her one last time. "Couple days at the most."

She got back in, and Sean waved to her while speaking quietly. "Billy, we've got company."

Billy spoke from the corner of his mouth, not looking up. "Tall dude, looks like they put a bear in a man's suit? Same one we saw pass us coming back from Montreal?"

"That's him."

"What are we gonna do?" Billy was frowning.

"Ask him why he's following us."

"What if he's got a gun?"

"Why would he have a gun?"

"I don't know. But he might."

"Great." Sean bit his lip. It was possible, after all.

"And he's bigger than you," Billy said.

"A lot."

"Yeah. You sure about this?"

"What else are we going to do? If he does have a weapon, we certainly don't want him in the terminal, with all those people."

"So we're gonna do it?" Billy still hadn't looked up.

"Yes. Pick up your bags, and we'll walk toward him. His coat's unzipped. I'll grab him and yank it down. Think you can put a wrist lock on him?"

"No problem."

They walked toward the man, talking to each other in French. Sean suddenly dropped his bag, and whipped the man's coat down his back and pushed him up against the wall, pinning him. The man's arms were restricted by the coat, and before he could react to push Sean away, Billy got hold of his wrist and twisted it into a painful joint lock.

Sean spoke quickly. "I'm with the National Security Bureau. Who are you and what do you want?"

The man struggled, but couldn't break free. Billy twisted downward, and the man winced, but said nothing.

"You'd better talk, or you'll be spending the night in a holding cell," said Sean.

"Would you please release my employee," came a sharp female voice, cracking like a whip. Sean shot her a glance. She wore a stylish fur, expensive-looking heels, and was attractive, probably in her mid-thirties. She exuded an air of power and confidence.

Sean's thoughts reeled. *What the hell?* "Ma'am, this man has been following us, and he needs to answer some questions about why."

"His name is Russell, and he's acting under my orders."

"And who are you?"

"Aren't you just the gentleman?" She had a slight smile on her face.

"You're about to be in a lot of trouble," said Sean.

"Oh, I doubt that."

"Interfering with government business is pretty serious."

"Pff. I do it all the time. I'm Doctor Lorna Stephenson. Perhaps you've heard of me?"

Sean had not, but he saw Billy's eyes go wide. "Afraid not. Got some ID?"

She rolled her eyes and sighed, but dug into a purse and flashed a license. "You've seen he's not a threat. Now will you let him go?"

"Is he going to behave himself?"

"I promise I won't let him tear you apart, which is what he wants to do right now."

Sean released his grip and stepped back, as Billy let go. The man hiked up his coat and flexed his wrist.

The woman studied Sean. "You're pretty good. Most people can't take Russell."

The big man flushed. "There's two of them."

"Yes, I know, dear boy, I can count."

Sean looked at her. "So what's with your hired help shadowing us? You've got some explaining to do."

"I suppose so," she said. "But why don't we do it inside, where it's warmer, and I can get some coffee?"

An airport security guard came up. "Is there a problem?"

Sean took a deep breath, the adrenaline starting to ebb. He flashed his ID. "National Security Bureau. We had some questions for this man, and she says he works for her."

The guard look at Stephenson. "Ma'am? Do I know you?"

She smiled, turning up the wattage. "I'm Doctor Lorna Stephenson. You watch TV?"

"Ah, yeah, that's it. Saw you on that documentary."

"And I was just about to explain why I'm here. But it's so cold."

Sean looked around, nodded. "All right. Let's go inside."

Inside the terminal, the woman put her hand on the guard's arm. "Do you mind if we sit while we do this? These heels are killing me. And I'd love to get something hot to drink."

The guard looked at Sean, who realized the woman had taken control of the situation and steered it to her advantage. He could play a hardass, but he held back for when he needed it.

Still holding onto the guard, Stephenson led the way, and sat at a table by a coffee shop. She looked up at the guard. "Will you stay right here and make sure these men aren't too rough with me? They look pretty mad."

The guard looked like he'd shoot Sean and Billy if she asked. They set down their bags and took chairs. The guard hooked his thumbs in his belt and stood by.

"That's better," Stephenson said. "Russell, be a dear and get me an Irish coffee, the good kind. You boys want anything?"

Sean and Billy shook their heads, and the big man left.

"Now he's going to sulk and be cranky all day, and I have you to thank."

"Doctor Stephenson—"

"Please," she said, looking into Sean's eyes as she touched his forearm. "Call me Lorna."

"I saw you on TV, too," Billy said.

Stephenson looked at him. "Well aren't you just the cutest thing?" She reached over and pinched his cheek. "Are you sure you wouldn't like some hot chocolate?"

Billy blushed furiously.

Sean frowned. "So why are you following us?"

She looked at Billy. "Tell your hunky friend here what I do."

"She's a cryptozoologist."

"Full marks," she said, favoring Billy with a smile. "Although he probably doesn't know a big word like that."

"It's a—"

"I know what it is," Sean didn't take his gaze from the woman. "That doesn't explain how you know who we are and why you're interested in us."

Stephenson smiled at the guard. "You've been a dear, and I thank you. But I'm about to reveal sensitive information, and these two would be in a lot of trouble if it got out. I think you've scared them into behaving."

The guard touched his cap. "No problem. Pleasure meeting you, Ma'am." He moved off.

Stephenson looked at the two. "You can cut the tough guy routine. I know you're here because of the Wendigo."

Sean sat for a moment and blinked, as he put it together. Unless there had been an information leak at the top, there was only one way she could have found out. "That was you upstairs at Atherton's?"

Stephenson merely smiled. "I sponsored the printing of his book."

"Why?"

"Are you really that dense?"

Sean frowned. "You think the Wendigo is real?"

"Of course it is. And I'm going to be the first to prove it."

"You can't be serious. It's just a legend, a myth."

"The legend is just an explanation for an actual creature."

"A creature? You think there's a huge living thing like that roaming the woods that we don't know about?"

"Oh, we know about it, we just haven't brought one back for study. Ever hear of the Yeti? How about the Sasquatch? Or skunk apes?"

"Sure, but—"

"All similar ideas, but different creatures. Many cultures have an analogous concept. It's just a large ape-hominid relative. Why is that so hard to believe?"

Stephenson didn't look up as Russell set down her drink. She took a sip and smiled.

"Little early for that, isn't it?" Sean said. "It's not even noon."

"You sound like my father. And that's not a compliment. Truth is, I've been up for about eight hours already, so I need a little pick-me-up."

"A bit driven, are we?" His jibe hit home, as a look of annoyance crossed the woman's face. "So why hasn't anyone caught one of these things yet?"

Stephenson waved her hand. "These are intelligent beings, and they're wary around humans. They live so far in the deep woods and uninhabited areas that they're only occasionally spotted. But we still have hundreds of documented sightings. Hundreds."

"There's hundreds of UFO sightings, too. And ghosts."

Stephenson eyed Sean. "You're trying to rile me up. People like you make me want to find one of these things even more."

Sean smiled. "And you'll be even more famous."

"I'll be vindicated," Stephenson said.

Sean nodded. "Must be hard, trying to convince people when they're laughing at you."

"They'll be laughing out the other side of their mouth soon enough. And that's why I'm going up there with you. To find the Wendigo and bring it back."

"You're not going anywhere with us."

"Really? You do realize I know exactly where you're going, and there's nothing you can do to stop me? Go ahead and call your Mr. Shepherd, who will call his boss, who will call his, who will then call the Prime Minister's office, where they will be informed that I'm the daughter of one of the P.M.'s oldest and dearest friends, the distinguished Professor Lawrence Stephenson. I'm sure even a flunkey like you has heard of him."

"I've heard of him," said Sean, not liking where this was going. "So what?"

"So I can go to the press, and tell the government the clusterfuck that follows was your fault. Your next assignment will be guarding a birdshit-covered island in northern Newfoundland."

Sean knew politics, and knew in his gut she was telling the truth. His bureau hated public scrutiny, and she could cause a media explosion. Her casual name-dropping indicated she had insider knowledge of certain government levels. She even knew Shepherd was his boss. He was decidedly uncomfortable with her. "I'm going to make some calls."

"Of course," she said, not unkindly. "Listen, I know you have your investigation to run, and I won't get in the way of that. You see the Wendigo as some fantastic story cooked up to explain a murder, but I know the thing is real, and I'm going to bring back a body to prove it."

"Don't you want it alive?

"Alive or dead, doesn't matter. What matters is that I bring back proof. It's a big area up there, and I don't want to risk it getting away." Stephenson sighed. "Listen, nothing against you two fine young lads, but my people are professionals, and can institute a big search far better than anything two junior field agents can do."

Sean opened his mouth to protest, but realized she had the advantage.

"Yes," she smiled at him. "I'm that resourceful. Only took me a few phone calls to track you from here to Thunder Bay to the north woods. But while you're eating your cardboard sandwich in tourist class on Air Canada, I'll have a gourmet luncheon on my private jet. Sure you don't want to join me? And I'll have my own helicopter fly us up from there. There's a hunting camp in the area, and my advance team is opening it up as we speak. Where were you staying again? As I recall, there's no Hiltons up there."

Sean looked at Billy, who only shrugged.

Stephenson finished her drink and checked her watch. "Looks like you boys better get to your gate, you'll be boarding in a minute. See you up north." She stood, and her tall companion rose as well. Sean watched them walk away.

"Can you believe that?" Billy shook his head. "She's not just one step ahead of us, we're not even on the same track."

"I'm going to call Shepherd. I don't know how she got all that confidential information."

"She could get anything she wants."

"Close your mouth Billy, you might catch some flies. Are you in love again?"

"Always. Think it's too late to get a ride on her jet?"

CHAPTER 10

The plane taxied out to the runway, lumbering like a giant beast along the concrete that had been scraped clean of most of the snow. At the head of the runway, the plane shuddered, as if in anticipation of its gravity-defying act. The big engines whined to a higher pitch as the craft gathered speed and finally leaped into the air.

Unwrapping a pack of gum, Sean popped a stick in his mouth, and offered one to Billy, who shook his head. Sean watched out the tiny window as they angled into the sky. Tall buildings shrunk to dollhouse size and smaller as they left Ottawa behind. Sean yawned and chewed his gum furiously to relieve the pressure in his ears from the change in altitude.

"Icarus," said Sean, looking out the window.

"What?"

Sean pointed. "The sun. We're flying too close. Our wings will melt."

"You're weird."

"Screw you. Read a book sometime. Like this one." Sean held up his copy of Atherton's book.

"As if."

Sean started reading. He was absorbed in the psychological aspects of the Wendigo legend when the flight attendants came around with lunch. Sean munched his dry sandwich as the plane plunged into massive cloud-banks, obscuring the view with a rolling white curtain. Droplets of moisture beaded on the window. Sean took a drink and swirled the ice around. How icy would it be, outside in that frigid air and whirling whiteness?

Billy tried to make small talk with the attendant when she came by. But she was all business and soon moved off. Billy shrugged, closed his eyes, and settled in for a nap.

Sean tried to read, but after a while the words on the page would not cohere into any meaning. He set the book down and looked at the whiteness outside until he drifted away.

Sean was in a world of white all around. He staggered and tried to call out, but here was no sound, nothing to see or touch. Then the whiteness parted, to show the prow of a boat. He was aboard then, and looked toward the back of the boat, where a hooded figure stood, poling the craft forward. Something shook him.

"What the hell?" Sean came to, Billy prodding him in the shoulder. Sean rubbed his eyes as the clouds parted and the cabin of the plane was flooded with dazzling sunlight.

"Check it out," Billy said, pointing to a dark expanse below. "Karen said that's Lake Superior."

"Charon?" Sean pronounced the name with the hard *k* sound. "The boatman on the Styx? I was dreaming about him."

"What the hell are you talking about?

"Charon. The ferryman who takes the dead across."

Billy laughed. "No, dummy, *Karen* is our stewardess. The cute one, not the battle-ax. Man, you were really out of it."

"They don't call them stewardesses anymore. And *you* were the one bringing up mythology."

"You're cranky when you get up from your nap."

Sean looked down to see puffs of cotton-candy leftovers casting wispy shadows on the endless inland sea. Huge transport ships were toy boats on the vast expanse of water, their wakes making widening vees behind them.

They gradually descended, until the massive tanker ships and freighters that supplied Thunder Bay grew larger and more detailed. Even in winter, the supplies had to get through. Tall grain elevators by the shoreline stood like castle towers of a magical kingdom. Sean had never seen it before, and marveled at how majestic it was.

The jet eased ever lower, approaching the ground with frightening speed. The wheels snagged the runway, jolting the big aircraft.

From the ground, the charms of Thunder Bay were hidden, and it looked like every other airport. As soon as the seat belt sign was off, people sprang up to stand in the aisle, as if they would get off quicker by doing so. Billy was one of them. Rather than stand and be jostled, Sean stayed seated and continued to read. It was a full fifteen minutes before the people started to move. When the crowd had cleared somewhat, Billy looked like he was dancing with impatience, and Sean finally got up.

Billy stopped to say goodbye to the flight attendant, nodding at Sean. "He thinks you transport the dead."

"Sometimes we do," the woman said, and Sean felt a stab of dread as they moved off the plane.

At the Northern Air desk they were directed back outside. Out on the tarmac, a helicopter waited. Sean had expected a floatplane with pontoon skis, something he had been in before, but this was outside his experience, and it made him uneasy.

An attendant was stuffing the last bags and packages into the back of the helicopter. Sean waited until he finished, and opened the passenger door. The chopper pilot was talking into his headset. He picked up a clipboard from the passenger seat, and pointed to Sean and Billy's names typed out on the paper. Sean nodded, and got an okay sign. Sean wedged his own bag in with the others in back, saw how small the space was, and looked at Billy.

"Sorry, partner, but no way I can fit back there."

Billy sighed and climbed in the back, wriggling around and moving things to fit into the seat. Sean squeezed into the passenger seat, which was still a bit too small for his large frame. He buckled the seat belt and got settled in as best he could.

The pilot ran through his checklist, and switched on the engine. The helicopter shuddered violently as the blades whipped around overhead, picking up speed.

Soon they lifted off, and Sean had the unsettling sensation of being in an upside-down lawnmower. While he had felt comfortable and safe enough on the big jet, being in the rocking, bouncing helicopter was like riding a leaf on the wind. The tiny craft hung precariously in the sky. Sean shivered, and attributed it to the cold air, mere inches away through the Plexiglas window.

Before long, they were flying over open wilderness, barren stretches without buildings or people. The vastness of the landscape gave Sean a thrill of exultation, and he was giddy with adrenaline. There was so much land below that it made him feel tiny and insignificant. He also noted that as he got farther from the city, his transportation was rolling backward in size, smaller and smaller, into something more primitive and dangerous.

Seeing the terrain below made him think back to the Jack London stories he had read as a boy. Tales of rugged, heroic, sometimes doomed men, struggling to make a mark in a cold, hostile land. Sean had always wanted to be like those adventurers, but now he felt apprehensive. He shifted in his hard seat, aware that nothing here would offer him comfort.

There was also beauty in this forbidding terrain. From time to time, Sean spotted some animals moving below. At one point, Billy poked him and leaned forward to shout.

"Reindeer! Look! Down there. Fucking reindeer for Christmas! How about that?"

Sean turned and cupped his hand to his mouth and shouted back. "They're caribou."

But Billy had leaned back already, and probably didn't care about the correction. Sean shrugged. If Billy wanted reindeer, let him have them.

Sean saw glinting points on the snow and ice that created a shimmering carpet of jewels. Rivers that flowed too fast to freeze were filigrees of silver trim, and the sunlight itself was gold, more than even Midas or Croesus had ever dreamed of. The crisp blue sky and tall evergreens formed a majestic panoply on the sheer stretches of whiteness below.

The beauty and enormous scale of the landscape was hypnotic, however, overwhelming the senses. For mile after mile it was the same, and forced one to come to terms with it. The engine noise in the cabin made casual conversation impossible, so Sean was a passive spectator, and the monotony eventually bludgeoned him into boredom. After a while, he fell into a doze.

He walked behind a spectral figure with an indistinct shape, along a magical road that writhed and shimmered like the slick skin of a massive snake. The shadowy figure pointed out a strange menagerie of beasts that grazed alongside the road. Like the land around them, many were beautiful. But some of the creatures had long, sharp teeth and hideous claws stained with blood. Sean turned to ask the figure a question, but it was gone.

Some of the creatures moved in his direction. Sean looked for a tree to climb to escape, but there was nothing, and the beasts moved in. A huge book appeared in his hands, and as he read from it, the creatures moved back. Soon they were gone, and he was floating on a body of water, in a small car. As he looked down in horror, he realized the car was filling with water as it began to sink.

A tap on the shoulder brought Sean to a groggy waking.

Billy shouted in his ear again. "You okay?"

Sean turned his head. "Yeah. Why?"

"You're sweating," Billy yelled back. "We're here."

Sean blinked and shook his head to clear it, seeing a Quonset hut down below in a clearing. They descended, snow blowing away in a circle from the landing area. Sean felt a jolt as the craft touched down.

PART II

CHAPTER 11

The cold slapped Sean's bare face and gripped him with icy arms. He gasped as the frozen air needled his lungs. He exhaled, vapor hanging like a ghost in the air.

A small clearing squatted in the midst of trees on all sides. One lone Quonset hut stood off to the side. A man came out and walked toward them. He appeared to be in his early sixties, but carried himself well. He was shorter than Sean, and stouter, but it was hard to tell just how much was him and how much was his thick parka. He was clean-shaven under the fur-lined hat, and looked as if the cold didn't bother him a bit.

Sean stuck a hand out. "Sean Laporte, and this is Billy Chretien. You must be Peter Carroway."

The man looked closely at them and frowned, leaving his hands in his parka pockets. "I told them to send me investigators with field experience." He shook his head. "And they send me a couple of goddamn kids." He turned and walked away.

Sean stood there dumbfounded, his hand still extended into empty air. He looked at Billy.

"Well, fuck you too," Billy said to the man's back.

Sean called out. "Hey! You've got bigger problems."

Carroway came back, his mouth set in a grim line. His blue eyes looked colder than the air. "Like what?"

"Like there's someone else that's going to be snooping around. So you might actually want to talk to us first."

"Someone else?"

"Doctor Lorna Stephenson. A cryptozoologist."

"And what in the name of sweet Jesus might that be?"

Billy spoke. "They look for creatures. You know, like the Loch Ness monster or the Wendigo."

"A monster hunter? Are you fucking kidding me?"

"I wish I was," said Sean. "We talked to a professor at McGill to get some background, and the next thing we knew, this woman was following us. She's determined to come hunt for this thing."

"How's she gonna do that?" Carroway snorted. "There aren't any damn hotels or restaurants up this way."

"She's rich, and said something about opening up a hunting camp nearby. She's got a team of people."

Carroway frowned. "Can't your bureau do something?"

"She's too well-connected, and she could blow the lid off our case. So she's got us by the short hairs."

"Unbelievable." Carroway rubbed his brow.

"Yeah. So now that we're here, we might as well see what we can do before she horns in, eh?"

The man eyed them. "Either of you boy scouts been in charge of a homicide investigation before?"

"No," Sean admitted. "I've been agent in charge on four cases, but no homicides."

"Well, nothing personal, son, but this is a murder. It's a different animal. What about you?" The man looked hard at Billy, who grinned back at him.

"I cracked the case of who was taking lunches out of the break room."

"You think this is a goddamn joke?"

Sean jumped in. "Billy doesn't react well to cold receptions. Maybe we're not what you're looking for, but we're the ones they sent. They're short-handed right now, but to tell the truth, I don't think there's *anyone* in our bureau that's dealt with something like this."

"You got that right." Carroway scuffed the snow at his feet. "Either of you speak French, at least?"

"Both of us."

"Well thank God for small miracles. You can talk to the Crees... If *they'll* talk to *you*."

Billy spoke to Sean. "So he got us to come all the way up here, just so people won't talk to us?"

"You can always go back," Carroway said.

"Look, Mister Carroway," said Sean. "I'm sorry we got off on the wrong foot. But we have a delicate situation, and a busybody who's about to make it a thousand times worse. Can't we join forces before this gets completely out of control?"

"Goddamn it." Carroway chewed his lip for a bit, then jerked a thumb at a four-wheel-drive International. "Stow your gear in there."

Sean looked at the vehicle, where a plow blade attachment mounted on the front looked like it could move mountains of snow. He nodded with approval at the thickly-studded snow tires, and when he opened the rear door, a jumble of equipment greeted him. Billy had to move a set of jumper cables, a toolbox, and a battery charger. Carroway got behind the wheel and started the engine.

"Looks like you've got a whole workshop in here," Billy said.

Carroway turned his head. "You get stuck out here in the winter without help, you die. Simple as that."

Sean spoke up. "Looks like you're prepared for anything."

"Thought I was, 'til a few days ago." Carroway shifted and started driving.

"How did you get involved in all this?"

Carroway exhaled. "Day it happened, I saw a column of smoke, went to check it out. The Crees and I always got along reasonably well, considering, but it was obvious when I went out they sure didn't want me there. They were hiding something, and nobody was talking. I followed the trail out to the clearing, and caught the smell." Carroway's face wrinkled in disgust. "Only one time before I ever smelled anything like that. Car accident, driver burned up inside the vehicle. You never forget that."

"What did you do?" Sean said.

"Well, I thought they'd all gone crazy. I was careful from that point on not to let anyone get behind me."

"You thought they might attack you?" Billy said.

"You get a bunch of guilty-looking people around the remains of a human barbecue, a smart man uses a little caution."

"What happened next?" Sean took off his gloves, as it was finally warm enough in the vehicle.

"I started laying down the law, telling them they better come forth with the killer, or the government was going to come tear the place apart and arrest all the men, take them away."

"And they believed you?"

"Why not? It's happened to them in the past. The government dumped them there, in the middle of nowhere, where it could forget about them."

Sean looked at Carroway. "You think they got a raw deal."

"Just like all the other native people on this continent. When it wasn't all-out genocide, it was oppression to the point of slow extermination."

"But not now."

Carroway snorted. "Yeah, now they're left to die quietly, of despair, alcoholism and neglect."

"Did they talk?"

"Not for some time. I had to threaten and browbeat them. I'm not proud of that."

"But they committed a murder."

"I keep telling myself that I was justified. You know something? In the eight years since I've known them, there's been one real fight. There's also been five suicides. They internalize their pain and hopelessness."

"That doesn't change the facts."

"No," Carroway said. "But it tells me they thought they had a damn good reason. One of their leaders is Walking Cloud. He looks ninety, but is probably only about sixty or so. Finally he said that he was the one to blame for this, that I should take him away and not the others. Shit. Offered himself up as sacrificial goat to the white man. If we took him away, put him in cell, away from his people and the land, he'd be dead inside a week."

Sean unzipped his parka. "Mr. Carroway—"

"For Chrissakes, call me Pete."

"Pete, then. How did this all start?"

"They let me know a member of the tribe went out with his son to get a Christmas tree. Kind of strange."

"How so?"

"Christmas is the whites' holiday. The Crees don't really celebrate it like we do. They must have got it from television, or from that sky pilot that worked with them years ago."

"What's a sky pilot?" Billy leaned forward.

"The priest. He's the reason they have English names, even though they speak French, when they're not speaking their own tongue. He baptized them and gave them names he could pronounce, and tried to get them speaking English, but they slipped back into their ways as soon as he was gone." Carroway smiled. "The names were recorded that way, though, for a government census, and they stuck. No one's come out to work with them since."

"Except you," Sean said.

Carroway looked at him. "I'm a special case. I draw a government pension anyway, so I might as well earn it."

"Our office was glad you were there to handle it. They could sure turn the heat up in Ottawa. And we were hoping to keep the press out of it."

"You don't have to tell me about those jackals," Carroway replied. "For a story like this, they'd be all over it, even if they had to come by dogsled. They'd splash blood on the front pages, and every nut case in the country would snowmobile up here, bothering the Crees. The Crees don't deserve that, even after what they did. But don't expect a warm welcome."

"As long as they don't shoot us," Billy smiled.

"No guarantees," Carroway said.

CHAPTER 12

Carroway's house was small, and completely surrounded by snowy trees. It had an attached garage that was almost bigger than the house itself. All was dark but for the feeble glow from a light over the door, a welcome beacon.

Carroway stopped in the driveway and got out. Pinned by the headlights, he reached down for the garage door handle and tugged upward. The big panel slid up to reveal the interior. He got back in the vehicle and pulled forward, shut off the engine, and left the headlights on while he got out again. He flicked a wall switch, flooding the place with light, pulled down the garage door from the inside, and turned off the headlights.

As Sean got his gear from the back, he saw two snowmobiles off to the side. One had the back end suspended by a chain hanging from a crossbeam. Behind it was a workbench scattered with tools. It seemed the kind of a place his father would have liked, one that belonged to a man who enjoyed fixing and building things.

Carroway pulled a cord from the bench and connected it to a plug hanging from the grill of the vehicle.

"I haven't seen that since I was a kid," said Sean.

"What's it for?" Billy said, hefting his bag.

"Current keeps the engine warm enough to avoid freezing, so the car will start in the morning."

"Jesus, you really gotta prepare for everything up here," said Billy.

Carroway opened the door leading to the house, without using a key.

"You don't lock your door?" Sean said.

Carroway laughed. "Who's out here to steal anything?"

"I can't imagine doing that in the city."

"This is a different world."

They stood in a small kitchen with a single sink, a sliver of countertop, a woodstove, a tiny refrigerator that looked older than Sean himself, a small, chipped red table, and three chairs.

"Goddamn, it's cold," said Billy.

"I'll build up the fire," said Carroway, pulling open the stove door. "It'll warm up soon."

"Sure the Christ hope so," muttered Billy.

Sean and Billy went into the next room. They set down their bags, and stood on a threadbare oval rug covering the center of the floor.

Carroway came in and added sticks to a second, bigger woodstove, over in the corner, and stirred the innards with a poker. He finished and stood up, rubbing his hands. Sean saw the sleeves of his plaid shirt rolled back over the thick forearms to reveal another layer of clothing beneath. No wonder he hadn't seemed cold.

"You boys want a beer?"

"God, yes, thanks," Billy said, and Sean nodded.

An ancient couch and chair were the only places to sit. Two large bookcases occupied one wall, and an end table held a well-used record player.

Billy looked puzzled. "Something's missing."

"No television," Sean smiled.

"How the hell does anyone live without one? Especially up here?"

"Don't know. Ree would have a decorating fit."

Carroway returned with three beers. Sean took off his coat and took the proffered beer, and Billy took his. Carroway tipped his bottle toward them and offered a toast. "Here's to doing the right thing."

"I'll drink to that," Sean agreed, giving Billy a look to squelch any remarks, and they all drank.

Carroway set down his beer and opened the woodstove door again, using the poker to stab at the kindling within. A rosy glow came from the interior, and Carroway added a few larger pieces of wood from a basket lying nearby, before closing the stove door.

"Ready for the Grand Tour?" Carroway pointed to the side. "That's my room there. One of you can have that other bedroom, and one of you gets the couch. That's pretty much it."

Billy looked from the couch to Sean and his mouth pulled up to the side. "Let me guess."

Sean shrugged. "That couch isn't long enough to fit me. Besides, you'll be closer to the fire, so you'll stay warm."

"You're all heart."

"Plenty of blankets," said Carroway. "And a sleeping bag, if you need it. So you shouldn't freeze."

"Where's the necessary room?" said Billy. "It was a long flight."

"Outside."

Billy looked stricken. You're kidding, right?"

Carroway just shook his head, and Sean laughed.

"Very funny. That door, I take it."

"Sometimes you have to jiggle the handle a bit," said Carroway. "But she works as required."

"We appreciate you opening your home like this," said Sean.

"Well, it ain't fancy, that's for sure. You like stew?"

"Yeah."

"Good, because that's what's for dinner."

While Carroway went to the kitchen, Sean took his gear into the bedroom. The bed was small, but still took up most of the room. With a chair and an old nightstand, that was the extent of furnishings. Sean set down his bags and hung his coat on the back of the door. A tiny window framed the dark outside. He felt as if he was being watched. He pulled the shade down and frowned at the confined space.

Sean took his turn in the bathroom. When he came out, he picked up his beer, took another swallow, and went to the bookcases to peruse the selection.

There was a good range and variety. He passed an approving eye over the authors, including the Canadian writers: Robertson Davies, Margaret Atwood, Giles Blunt, and Farley Mowat. He saw a thick volume of the collected works of Shakespeare, a copy of Bulfinch's Mythology, a few poetry selections, some outdoor and nature books, crime and psychology books, and a few dozen novels.

"Yeah, I figured you'd be checking out the books," said Billy.

"You should try reading sometime."

"Nah. Hurts your brain."

They stood in the doorway to the kitchen while Carroway prepared the meal. When it was ready, Carroway served the stew into three bowls, and set them at the tiny table. He put out a box of crackers.

"I'm not much company," Carroway said. "Don't get many visitors. But I suppose we should make the most of it."

Billy grinned. "I was worried you'd be one of those recluses who talks someone's ear off as soon as they find a person to listen."

After dinner, Carroway washed up. Then he set out a bottle of blended Canadian whiskey, and they played cards for a bit. Sean kept cocking his ear for the usual sounds of household electronic devices ticking, of traffic, of music or television chatter, or other people, but there was nothing. The feeling of isolation was intense, and the silence was absolute, almost a palpable living thing.

CHAPTER 13

Sean was in darkness, floating on a long, narrow boat. He put his hand over the side and felt icy water chill his body. Carroway stood at the other end of the craft, dressed in a hooded robe, pulled up so that only his face showed. He held a long slender pole trailing off into the black water.

"Styx and stones," murmured Sean. He saw nearby icebergs that turned into corpses, bloated and pale white, showing horrible wounds. Some of the corpses moaned and drifted closer.

"Watch out!" Carroway cried out. "They're from the government!"

The bodies were now touching the boat, bobbing in the black water. Hands reached up, like supplicating lepers appealing to Jesus. Sean recoiled, fearing to touch them. He stood up in the boat, lost his balance, and pitched over the side.

Sean jerked awake and saw the ceiling overhead. He lay tense and rigid, breathing heavily. Disoriented, he looked around and finally remembered where he was. The room was wanly illuminated by a dull, unfriendly grayness, diffused through the thick frost on the window. He shook his head and tried to relax, but the residue of the dream still lingered. Sean pushed back the blanket and swung his feet to the floor.

"Jesus!" He gasped, jerking his feet away from the frigid wooden floorboards. Now fully awakened by the chill, he hooked his foot into a nearby throw rug and pulled it to the bed. With this as a buffer between his flesh and the cold floor, he dressed quickly. Armed against the cold, he made his way to the bathroom. Billy was still asleep on the couch, burrowed in so only his hair showed.

When Sean came out, he smelled the rich, homey aroma of fresh-brewed coffee, and followed it to the welcoming warmth of the kitchen. The small kitchen stove radiated heat, and Sean was glad to get near it. Carroway nodded to him by way of greeting and lifted the pot. Sean nodded assent, and Carroway poured coffee into a ceramic mug. He passed it to Sean, who gratefully took the mug and cupped his hands to feel the warmth.

"Milk and sugar on the table there," Carroway said.

"I had some pretty strange dreams."

"Oh?"

"I was in a boat. It was dark. It might have been the river Styx. I looked up, and you were steering."

"Charon the ferryman, huh?" Carroway looked amused. "Can't be me, I refused to enter the boating business. Interesting, though, that you were going to the land of the dead."

"My dreams aren't normally like that."

"Most people can't remember their dreams."

"When they're like that, I know why." Sean said. "By the way, your floor is mighty damn cold. If it hadn't been for that throw rug, I'd still be there."

"Wakes you up, don't it?" Carroway laughed. "You might want to go poke Sleeping Beauty. Breakfast is almost ready."

Sean went out and woke Billy.

"Whuh?" Came a voice from inside the blankets.

"Breakfast."

"Is there coffee?"

"Yes."

"'K."

Sean went back out to the kitchen, sat, and sipped his coffee, slowly coming to life. Billy joined them, and got a filled cup in front of him. He gave a thumbs-up sign without speaking.

Before long, Sean looked down at a plate with two slices of toast, and a bowl containing a steaming, grayish- brown mass. He stared at it.

"Oatmeal," Carroway said.

"Looks like shit," Billy said.

"Put a little of that maple syrup on it and a splash of milk," said Carroway.

"You first," Billy said to Sean.

Sean shook his head, but did as Carroway suggested. He stirred it around, took a tentative spoonful, and was surprised to find it quite tasty. He took a bite of toast, and swallowed some coffee. The whole combination warmed him. Billy, who had been watching him, now followed suit.

Carroway was filling a Thermos jug with the rest of the coffee. He took sandwiches out of the refrigerator and packed them in a cloth sack. "We'll probably be out the rest of the day. You'll want to dress warm."

Sean went to change, and took care to get the layers on properly. He knew the importance of dressing for extremely cold weather. He bundled his knit cap, good gloves, and ski jacket, and went back out. Billy was ready as well, wearing a hat with a pom-pom on top and strings hanging down the side.

"I had a hat like that, when I was seven," said Sean.

"This is the height of fashion," said Billy.

Carroway took his bundles, and shook his head when he spied Billy's headgear. They went out to the garage, and the cold air once again slapped Sean's exposed face. He pulled up the garage door as Carroway started the engine. Exhaust from the vehicle rolled out in huge white puffs in the icy air.

Carroway revved the engine after letting it warm up, and it settled into a smooth idle. He backed out of the garage, and Sean rolled down the garage door, got in, and took off his gloves.

"If you had an automatic garage door opener, you'd make your life a lot easier," Sean said.

"I need the exercise," grunted Carroway. "Keeps me in shape."

"Anyone else live nearby?"

"About ten kilometers or so thataway," Carroway gestured.

"And to think Trudeau was worried we were turning into 'a loose confederation of shopping malls'. This is too much space for me," said Sean. "Who plows the roads?"

"The lumber and mining companies. They keep it clear for the big trucks."

"Any other businesses?"

"Not a one. That's why the government put the Crees out here, because there's nothing else. If they ever did find a way to make this land pay, they'd come in and move the Crees again. Maybe to Baffin Island." Carroway downshifted and continued. "It's remote up here, but I like it. It's unspoiled. Back where I grew up, they even ruined the sea."

"Where was that?"

"Prince Edward Island. My family were all fishermen, and I worked on the boats with them. But no one can make a living fishing on the small boats anymore. The big factory ships come through and take all the fish. They've even stripped the Grand Banks. I left when I was eighteen, so I wouldn't get trapped into spending my life scouring for scraps."

"Aren't you supposed to miss the sea? You're about as far away as you can get."

Carroway laughed. "The truth is, there's a resemblance. When you flew in, what did you see?"

"About a million miles of open space."

"Yup. A broad expanse with no people. A place of mystery, of raw nature, where man is only a visitor."

Sean nodded, glad that Billy hadn't chimed in with a quip.

Carroway went on. "I'd left the shore for the city, and found Helen. When she died, years later, there was a big hole left behind. Drinking didn't help, just made me less able to deal with the pain. I wanted nothing more to do with people, and came up north to get away." Carroway seemed to reach back in memory as he spoke. "When I got up here, I was amazed. All this open land, and almost no one on it. It doesn't care what your problems are. You have to deal with it every day. No room for self-pity. In the quiet hours, you sort things out and put the stuff away that doesn't help you."

"Have the Crees found their peace?"

"I don't know," said Carroway. "I doubt they'd tell you. They just want to be left alone. Any idea what Ottawa wants to do with them?"

"The fact they sent us here is a good sign. They'd like to keep it quiet and see what we turn up. Be glad they didn't descend on you like the Wrath of God, with the whole crime lab and the specialty teams."

"Would have been funny, as there's no place to stay," Carroway chuckled. "They'd have been stacked up like cord wood."

"They'd have brought their own housing units. Would have cost the taxpayers millions. Thanks be to budget cuts."

"You can tell them when you get back to stop sending so much snow our way. It came early this year, and has really piled up. Worst winter since I've been here, that's for sure."

"So what do you do for fun around here?" said Billy.

"Ice fishing and snowmobiling, cross-country skiing, and snowshoeing. And we read a lot."

"No dogsleds?"

"Too many trees," said Carroway. "The dogs would have to stop every few feet to mark their territory."

"We have festivals in the city to get people through the winter," said Sean. "If only the sun was out. Makes things so gloomy."

"That's how it is, for months on end. You get used to it."

Sean did not think he would. He was acutely aware of missing Ree, and of missing other people. He stirred in his seat.

"What else can you tell me about this Whitefeather?"

"He and his wife lived in a cabin on the edge of Reserve land, away from the rest of the tribe. He hunted, fished, ran some traps."

"All legal?"

Carroway looked at Sean. "Does it matter?"

"I suppose not. Sorry, force of habit. Go on."

"That's it. I didn't really know him, since he kept apart from the others."

"Not a lot to go on."

"Nope."

"What about the other man he killed? Any history there?"

"Nothing I know about. Way the Crees talked, it was a random thing."

The trees close by the side of the road formed an endless corridor of sensory deprivation that eventually produced boredom. Sean was glad when they finally turned onto a crossroad. This road was not as well plowed, and the ride grew bumpy.

Carroway coughed. "What about this monster hunter you were telling me about?"

"She surprised the hell out of us," Sean said. "Had a guy following us, and when we jumped him, she was right there. Father's a pal of the P.M. I called my office, and they said to let her be."

"Why is she sticking her nose in this?"

"She thinks the Wendigo is some kind of real living creature. Like a Sasquatch."

Carroway snorted. "I've been up here eight years, and I haven't seen anything like that."

"She thinks she can find it."

"Just what we need," Carroway sighed. "Bunch of damn tourists traipsing through the woods while we investigate a murder."

"She can be a real pain in the ass, too."

"Well, let's get done what we can before she shows up with a circus. There's the Reserve."

Sean saw the weathered sign fixed over the road, and several 'Private Property—No Trespassing' warnings. "Those signs are up in the trees some, aren't they?"

"Any lower, they'd be covered in snow."

"It gets that high?"

"Bet your ass."

They bounced down the bumpy road for a time, until they came to a clearing with a cluster of buildings. Carroway parked and they got out.

Two Cree men came out of a building and walked toward them. Each carried a rifle.

"Looks like we've got a reception committee," said Billy.

CHAPTER 14

The bigger of the two Crees wore a red-and-black plaid hunting jacket, and a dark knit cap. The other was younger, and wore no hat, his long, loose black hair being lashed by the wind. They drew closer, and Sean saw their faces. The older man was impassive, showing nothing, but the younger man glared at them.

"Billy," Sean said. "When we get out, don't stand too close to me."

"You don't think they're going to shoot us?"

"I don't know what they're going to do. But they're standing there with rifles."

"And take that goddamned silly hat off," Carroway said. "They already hate us enough."

They got out. The only exchange of greeting was Carroway nodding to the Crees. The younger one spat. The bigger man jerked his head, indicating that they should follow.

Sean saw no one else about as they walked, but felt unseen eyes watching them, making a cold, prickly patch on the back of his neck. The two Crees took them into what looked like a bare-bones meeting hall, with tables and chairs stacked against a far wall. A stove by the near wall offered warmth, wood crackling inside it. The air had a musty smell.

Seated in a rocking chair by the stove was an old, white-haired Cree. He had on a coat, and his lower half was covered with a blanket.

The old man watched without comment as Carroway, Sean, and Billy unzipped their coats. The plaid-jacketed Cree opened the grey door of the stove and pushed in a piece of firewood. Sean saw the bright blaze from within. The two chaperones stepped out of earshot to the side, set their rifles against the wall, and stood with arms folded across their chests. The younger one still looked angry.

Carroway bowed his head slightly as he addressed the old man. "Walking Cloud, this man is Sean Laporte and this is Billy Chretien, representing the Government of Canada. Gentlemen, this is Walking Cloud, elder of the Cree Nation and representative of these people."

The old man nodded. He motioned for them to sit. When they were settled, the old man gave Sean a sharp look, who returned the gaze without challenge or submission. Sean felt as if the man was peering into his soul to ascertain his character. Walking Cloud's face was placid, with an ancient calm, and a demeanor of quiet dignity.

Sean greeted him in French, to which the man replied in a clear, unwavering voice. His accent was easily understandable. Sean took out his notebook and pen and laid them on the table, and kept his questions in French.

"You understand why I must ask you these questions?"

Walking Cloud nodded.

"Could you tell me what happened that day?"

"One of our young ones had gone out with his father on one of the snow machines. The young one returned alone, saying they had been attacked. Our men went out, and followed the trail to the cabin of Whitefeather. They found the bodies of the boy's father, and of Whitefeather's woman. The men brought Whitefeather back and asked what must be done.

"He had been taken over by the Wendigo, so we built a fire the next day and drove the spirit from him."

Walking Cloud cleared his throat and went on. "Do not punish my people, for I was the one to counsel the deed. We have kept to the old ways. Take me to your jail, but leave my people be. We have suffered enough, for the Wendigo has already taken three of us this winter."

"Did you see the bodies?"

"I did," said Walking Cloud. "They bore the marks."

"Could it have been a bear, a wolf, or some other animal?"

Walking Cloud looked at him. "I know what the marks of wolves and bears are like. These were the marks of a man."

Sean tapped his pen. "Did Whitefeather say anything?"

"I spoke to him, but the Wendigo does not answer. It was in his eyes, for all to see. He was like an animal."

"Were you angry at him for killing those people?"

Walking Cloud shook his head. "It was not Whitefeather who killed our people, but the demon. I have no anger in my heart, but there is a heavy sadness that the Wendigo is among us, stalking our people."

"How do you know the spirit was driven out of Whitefeather?"

"It was in the smoke of the fire."

Sean looked at Billy and then back. "What did it look like?"

"What does the wind look like? I can tell you how it moves the leaves of the trees, or how it makes waves upon the waters, but I cannot put a hat on it and take a picture."

Sean smiled in spite of himself. He sensed the old man was not trying to be deliberately evasive, but the truth was as elusive as grabbing for a cloud. He spread his hands. "Where did it go?"

"I do not think it has gone far."

"Was there a point where the spirit was driven out, and you could have saved Whitefeather?"

"He had been saved."

"I meant his body."

Walking Cloud shook his head. "His body was not as important as his spirit."

"Perhaps it was to him," said Billy.

"Perhaps," Walking Cloud looked at Billy before turning back to Sean. "But he had eaten the flesh of his people, and the Wendigo could return and make him kill again."

Sean looked at Walking Cloud. "What do you do at other times when a member of your tribe kills another member?"

"That has not happened in many, many years."

"What if Whitefeather had killed his wife and the other man, but not been possessed by the Wendigo?"

"We would have held council and decided what to do."

"Would you have turned him over to the authorities?"

"Which authorities?"

"The government." Sean leaned forward a bit.

"Ah. The men who rule in the faraway city. I do not know. Your law is hard for us to understand."

"Why is that?"

"Since the coming of your people many generations ago, one of you kills a Cree, and your law does nothing. We were brought here so we would not be in the way of your people. Our people sicken and die, and there is nothing. So why do you now care if a Cree kills another Cree?"

Sean tapped his pen on the table. "In the past, many wrongs were done to your people, and men kept the law from protecting you. But now the law protects everyone, and it says that it is wrong for any man to kill another. All the people of our nation must live by this law. When a man kills another man, he must stand trial, and if he is guilty, he must be punished."

"What would your law have done to Whitefeather?"

"He would have been taken away, and your people would have had nothing to fear from him."

"And what of the Wendigo?" Walking Cloud's face was serious. "What does your law say of that?"

"The law deals with the world of men, and how they behave toward one another. It does not deal with the world of spirits."

"Then your law would not have helped Whitefeather. He would have died with the Wendigo still possessing him."

"There are doctors who might have been able to help him."

Walking Cloud smiled. "Ah, yes, the doctors that see into the minds of men. Tell me, do they deal with the world of the spirits?"

"They believe the spirits are created by the minds of men. If they can change the minds of men, they can drive those spirits out."

Walking Cloud nodded. "Then yes, I believe they can help the people of your world. But those who do not believe in the Wendigo can never drive it away. It is ancient and powerful, and was here long before your people came." Walking Cloud looked at Sean sternly, but not unkindly.

"Your law cannot help us, and you cannot help us. Nothing from your world can. From the time the first of your people came to us, you bring us death whenever and wherever you come. We do not want to change, to be part of your world.

"You say we must all live under the laws of the whites. But why does the white man not live under the laws of the Crees, which are older, and make far more sense? We will live and die here by the ways of our fathers. We can do no more."

Sean sat back, not knowing what to say. Walking Cloud had, without anger, repudiated the authority and sovereignty of the Canadian government.

Noise erupted from outside. The two Crees grabbed their rifles and went to check out the source. Carroway got up and went to the window. "Now who in the hell could that be?"

Sean and Billy looked at each other. "Oh, shit," said Billy.

CHAPTER 15

Sean and Billy rose and went to the window. Three large black SUVs occupied the square alongside Carroway's International. They were huge vehicles, with chains on their tires. Each had a trailer carrying a pair of new snowmobiles. Several non-native men were passing out something to a group of Crees who had gathered.

Billy laughed. "Look at her, arguing with those two Crees with rifles. Her bodyguard looks like he wants to charge in and tackle them, guns or no."

Sean saw her put a hand on the arm of the hulking Russell, much like someone would take the collar of a dog about to attack. "I better get out there, before someone gets killed." He put on his coat and went outside. Billy joined him a moment later, while Carroway beat them both to the disturbance.

"What the hell's all this?" Carroway's voice cut through the cold air.

Stephenson looked at him calmly and cleared her throat. "My men were just distributing a few extra supplies we brought with us. And I wanted to have a talk with their head man."

"You can't come here like this."

"Except for those two guard dogs, they don't seem to mind," Stephenson indicated the smiling group of women and children with arms full of packages.

"Well, *I* mind," said Carroway. "And I'm the law up here, so get back in your vehicles and clear out."

"You have no jurisdiction here, Mr. Carroway. This is Cree land, and you're as much a guest as I am."

"How the hell do you know my name?"

"Don't look so shocked. A few phone calls. How do you think I got here?"

"You better not piss me off, lady."

"Or what? You'll arrest me? We both know that's not going to happen. Stop wasting time, so we can get on the trail of this Wendigo."

"The trail? What *trail*? The Wendigo is a myth."

"Not to these people.

"These people..." Carroway looked around and threw up his hands. "What are you going to do? Ride around the woods on those snow machines, looking for a goddamn mythical being?"

"Do you have a better idea?"

"Yeah. Why don't you get your ass in that vehicle and take your fancy circus back to wherever you came from?"

Sean noticed the bodyguard take a step forward, and moved in to keep the peace. He saw that the two Crees had backed off, and both were smiling. Sure. The white government men were being shown up by a woman. Laugh it up, boys.

"Let's go inside," said Stephenson. She looked at Sean. "Here we go again."

Sean shrugged as Carroway looked at him. They trooped inside, and Stephenson was introduced to Walking Cloud.

She wasted no time addressing the older man, speaking in perfect French. "When did you first hear of the Wendigo?"

"From the time of my first rememberings."

"Were there any other encounters with your people?"

"When I was young, we did have such a one. It was a winter such as this, and there was little to eat. One man tried to kill another when he was possessed by the Wendigo, but he was stopped. The ceremony was held, and the Wendigo driven from him. He survived, and lived for many years."

"What?" Sean broke in. "He survived a burning?"

"No. He had not killed, so we were able to drive the Wendigo from him. It is not always so."

"Were you present? Did you actually see this happen?"

"I saw the ceremonies. We were prepared, and had been watching, because we had seen the marks of the Wendigo in the forest that winter."

"Marks?" Stephenson leaned forward. "What kind of marks?"

"Tracks. It was like the foot of a man, but much larger. It walked on two legs, and would have been as tall as you and another half your height."

"See?" Stephenson said. "They think of it as a spirit, but acknowledge that it takes physical form."

Sean spoke. "Could it have been made by men? Perhaps someone playing a joke?"

"None could have and none would. This is not a place where we play tricks with our lives."

"Did anyone else see these tracks?" Stephenson sounded excited, her eyes shining.

"Yes."

Sean was irritated with Stephenson's interruptions. "What did you do then, when you thought the Wendigo was about?"

"If we went into the forest, we went in groups. The way of the Wendigo is to take one man at a time."

"You didn't try to hunt it?"

"To what purpose? How do you kill a demon?" Walking Cloud smiled slightly.

Sean smiled back. "I see your point. So winter is the only time when the Wendigo walks?"

"It is strongest then. So now our people will not go out alone this winter."

Walking Cloud looked down. "Are you going to take me away now? I would like to say goodbye to my people."

Sean blinked. "We're not taking anyone just yet. We need to talk to the other men who found Whitefeather. And the boy."

"These two were in that group," Walking Cloud gestured to the two men who stood to the side. The boy is young and can tell you nothing."

"Maybe not, but we need to speak to him."

"He suffers from his father's death."

"We will try to cause as little pain as possible."

Walking Cloud nodded, and motioned the older man over, speaking rapidly in the Cree tongue. The man left, and Walking Cloud signaled for the other man to come and sit. He was still surly, but Walking Cloud bade him answer Sean's questions, which he did with little embellishment. Sean got monosyllabic responses and a similar story to what Walking Cloud had told him.

The other man returned with a wide-eyed boy, who turned pale at seeing the crowd of strange adults. Sean asked him a question, but boy broke down and cried. Walking Cloud spoke sharply to him, and the tears stopped, but the boy was silent.

Stephenson stepped forward. "Let me handle this." She whispered to Russell, then squatted and smiled at the boy, and spoke to him in French. She reached behind his ear and brought forth a coin and held it up before him. The boy stared at it, eyes widening. She reached behind his other ear and brought forth another. His mouth opened, and she handed him the coins. He looked up at her. Russell held a Thermos bottle in one hand and handed her a steaming cup. She offered it to the boy, and led him to a seat. The boy sniffed at the contents of the cup, blew on it, and took a tentative sip. He smiled, and Stephenson ruffled his hair. She let him drink a bit before she spoke. When she did, her voice was soft, her tone gentle. The boy was hesitant, but she coaxed him into answering, and he eventually confirmed all that Walking Cloud had said, but without adding anything new.

She looked at the men and shrugged. Sean nodded. The larger man took the boy away.

Carroway stretched. "Now what?"

Sean looked around. "We talk to the men who went out to capture Whitefeather."

The men were brought over one at a time, and all told a similar story. Sean and Billy tried to root out any inconsistencies, but there was nothing amiss.

"That's the last one," said Billy. "Now what?"

Sean put away his notes. "I don't know, but my throat's dry."

"Try a nip of this," Stephenson said, passing over a flask.

Sean sipped, and got a mouthful of good Canadian whiskey. He passed it back, but she didn't offer it to anyone else. "I hope that's not what you gave the kid."

She laughed. "Of course not. But all kids like hot chocolate."

"That was a neat technique with the coins."

"It pays to have a trick or two up your sleeve."

"What else do you need?" Carroway said to Sean, ignoring Stephenson.

"I want to see where they burned Whitefeather."

They stood up and put on their coats, nodded to Walking Cloud, and went outside. The wind slapped against them.

"It's this way," said Carroway, and started down a trampled trail.

Having two armed men behind him made Sean nervous. "One thing's for sure," he said. "They believe in this thing, and are convinced they had a demon among them."

"Hell of a thing," Billy said. "Believing in demons."

"Ain't it the truth," Carroway agreed. "Clearing's up ahead here."

The snow crunched under their tread, and Sean felt as if he was walking on bones. They came upon a clearing with a flat blackened area, with heaped ashes still visible, despite the snow that had fallen since the incident.

Sean scuffed at the ashy remains. He walked the perimeter, squinting at distances, mentally measuring and calculating. He approached the charred stump in the middle and squatted to inspect it, poking with a stick. Stephenson and Russell stayed back, letting him do his thing. Stephenson furiously puffed on a cigarette.

There was a kind of uneasy feel to this place, as if spirits did indeed reside. Sean closed his eyes and heard the crackle of flame, the feel of the heat. He felt a presence, just beyond the reach of his conscious mind. He opened his eyes and blinked, looking around.

"Hey, Major Tom. You okay?" Billy said.

"Yeah, sure. Just thinking."

"Anything else you want to see here?"

"No, we're done."

They retraced their path to the main hall.

"Now what?"

"We're going to start a search pattern," said Stephenson. "Take these snowmobiles and head out to where they picked up Whitefeather."

"Now that'd be pretty stupid," said Carroway.

She turned on him, her mouth small and tight. "And why's that?"

Carroway smiled. "You feel that? Wind's picking up. There's a storm moving in. You take you people out on snowmobiles, you'll get caught, and someone will die."

"We're not afraid of a little snow." Russell's voice was a low rumble.

"Guess you've never been in whiteout conditions, then. You can be even a few feet apart and lose sight of each other. You won't be able to see a damn thing. Won't be able to find your way back, and you'll freeze to death."

The two men glared at each other.

Stephenson spoke up. "Well, we wouldn't want that now, would we? How about some lunch, then? Gentlemen, would you like to come to my camp? I'm sure I can offer you better hospitality than even Mr. Carroway's cozy cabin."

They all got in their respective vehicles and Carroway went last, following Stephenson's party. The two watchful Crees kept their gaze upon them until they could no longer be seen.

Sean slumped in his seat and let out a sigh.

"What's the matter?" Billy said.

"This would be a lot easier if it was a straightforward murder. Either the wife or the man. Both, that's no sane motive."

"Unless they were having an affair," said Billy.

"Don't try to put sane motives from our world onto this," Carroway said.

"I just never understood crazy people," said Sean.

"It helps to be one," said Billy.

CHAPTER 16

"Well, isn't this cozy?" Billy laughed as they pulled into a cleared space in front of a large, two-story hunting camp. Through the windows, people could be seen moving around the well-lit interior, and smoke rose from two chimneys. "Nothing against your place, Pete, but it looks like she's got a little more room."

Carroway shook his head. "Some rich goddamned idiot wanted to build his own palace out here, be king of the wilderness or something. Wouldn't listen when they told him the hunting wasn't good, that he'd have better luck elsewhere. Went ahead, and this place has sat idle for the most part. Don't know how she found it."

Sean looked at the cheerily-lit place, so much bigger and brighter than Carroway's. "She seems to be rather resourceful."

"That what you call it?" Carroway had a sour look on his face. "My terminology would be less polite."

"She's pushy, but at least we don't have the press up here. She could have called them."

"Probably didn't want them laughing at her. Tracking something that doesn't exist. What an idiot."

"I suppose we'd better go in."

They got out and walked up to the porch, clumping the snow from their boots. A scowling Russell opened the door and stood aside to let them in.

They gaped at the scene before them, with half a dozen people engaged in various tasks.

"A chandelier," said Sean. "An honest-to-God chandelier in a hunting camp."

"Check out those deer heads on the wall," said Billy. "Looks like he bagged a whole herd. And how about those mounted fish?" He shook his head. "I couldn't even tell what kind some of them are. I thought you said the hunting wasn't that good?"

"Way I heard tell," said Carroway. "He bought all that from somewhere else and brought it here. Some of those fish you won't find in any lake or river. Don't know if he didn't know the difference between ocean catch and inland fish, or he didn't care."

"Would you look at the maps?" Billy sounded awed. "She must have the whole province gridded out on that wall."

"Hello, boys," Stephenson walked up to them, cigarette in one hand, and a glass in the other. "Like my home away from home?"

Sean couldn't help himself. "The chandelier's a nice touch."

Stephenson laughed. "I do so love the follies of rich assholes. Don't you?"

Even Carroway smiled.

"How about some lunch? I told my chef there would be a few guests. We'll eat in the other room. Don't want to get in the way of the worker bees."

"They're not joining us?"

Stephenson gave Sean a look. "God, we don't eat with the *help*. Honestly." She walked away, and the men followed her to a huge kitchen area, with a large table in a dining alcove.

"Take a seat," she said. "I need a refill. Russell, be a dear and see if the lads want anything to drink."

The big man looked at her, but stood by the table and waited.

"I'll have a Mai Tai," said Billy. "And can you put one of those little umbrellas in it, and some fruit on a plastic sword?"

"Behave, Billy," said Sean.

"Fine. I'll have a beer, then."

Sean and Carroway agreed to coffee, and Russell moved off to get their drinks.

Billy looked thoughtful. "Do you think Russell's his first name, or his last?"

"He don't talk much, does he?" Carroway said.

"Tough for him to form words," said Billy. "Makes his brain hurt."

Stephenson joined them, a tall iced glass in her hand. "Well, that went well today. You boys get what you need?"

Sean shrugged. "We've got a triple murder, and a group of people right out of the past, killing one of their own for a legend. What the hell do we do with that?"

"Catch the damn thing, so no one else gets blamed for becoming one." Stephenson set down her glass and lit another cigarette.

"Catch it. So you chase monsters," Carroway said. "How does someone get into a hobby like that?"

Stephenson eyed him coolly. "By having an asshole for a father, who's also the most literal-minded scientist ever. If he can't test it in a lab, it doesn't exist. He's on a board that publishes books and articles explaining and disproving all sorts of phenomena. I only have to find one thing he says doesn't exist. One black swan, so to speak, to negate his entire life's work." Stephenson took a drag from her cigarette. "Oh, don't you all look at me like that. I know what you're thinking. Sure, I've got issues. We all do. Take Billy here. He'll probably be thinking of me naked next time he masturbates."

Stephenson patted a furiously blushing Billy on the head and laughed. "I mean, look, I've got two doctorates, and the sonofabitch tried to have me declared mentally incompetent. Said my work was demonstrable evidence of impaired cognitive ability."

A man entered from the other room. "Excuse me, Doctor Stephenson—"

"Chuck, come in, come in. Boys, meet Chuck, my cameraman. We're making this hunt a documentary. What's up, Chuck? Get it? *Upchuck?*" Stephenson looked at the men, who stared back at her. "Okay, tough crowd. What do you have for me, Chuck? Good news, I hope."

"They said to tell you the storm's moved in, but it should be over by tomorrow."

"Well, that is good news. Looks like you were right, Carroway. Good nose for weather. Looks like we'll be stuck here until tomorrow."

"We'd better get going, then," Carroway said, standing up.

"Oh, stay. Here's your food. It would be rude to leave now, and you don't want to go away hungry."

Carroway looked at Sean and Billy, who both shrugged. He nodded and sat back down.

What Stephenson had served to them for a casual field lunch would have sufficed for a gourmet feast at one of Ottawa's finest restaurants. The three men ate with gusto.

"Get enough?" Stephenson asked, when they'd finished.

"Impressive," said Sean. "I see you like to travel in style."

"If you can't enjoy wealth, then what's the point of having it? You boys will want to be around for the celebration after we catch the thing. I've got a bottle of nice champagne we're going to break open that cost me three thousand dollars."

"What makes you so sure the Wendigo is real?" Sean looked at her.

"I've been studying these things for a long time. There's too much evidence to ignore: sightings, tracks, everything. The Crees are the perfect credible witnesses, not prone to instituting a hoax on the outside world. The last thing on earth they want is for a screaming bunch of reporters flooding onto their land. Their people discovered something out there, and we're going to run it to ground."

"That's a lot of ground to cover," said Carroway. "If it's kept secret for this long, how are you going to find it?"

Stephenson laughed. "You did see the equipment in the other room, didn't you? We call it the War Room. We've got photos, satellite phones for communication, maps of every square inch for a thousand miles. We're getting a tracking dog team in, and we'll have aerial reconnaissance radioing down to the ground crews. We'll have teams out on snowmobiles, and we'll set up checkpoints when we've cleared areas. A winter like this, the thing will need food, need to go ranging for it."

"What does it eat?"

"Whatever it can, this time of year. We're bound to run across it."

"What will you do when you find it?"

"We'll open that champagne, and we'll take it back to civilization, where I can rub my father's nose in it for the rest of his miserable life. And I'll be the most famous rich bitch around. If we take it alive, we'll take it on a world tour while we study it, show it to the whole fucking planet. The eighth wonder of the world."

"Like King Kong," said Billy. "That didn't turn out so well, I hear."

Stephenson gave him a look. "Well, once I get it back, I don't give a shit if it *does* escape and climb the Empire State Building."

CHAPTER 17

Stephenson gathered everyone into the central area. She stood under the chandelier, with a cigarette in one hand and a large glass of blood-red wine in the other. She motioned with her hands, and Sean was transfixed, wondering when the wine would spill. She explained in detail the particulars of the search that would commence as soon as the storm was past.

Sean thought that she seemed to love telling everyone what they would be doing as part of her grand plan, moving everyone around like chess pieces.

"All right," she said. "Let's get back to work."

There was a bustle as Stephenson's crew returned to their charts and grids and logistics. She approached the three men.

Carroway spoke up. "You seem to be under the impression we *all* work for you. You go off on your wild goose chase and have fun. But we've still got an investigation to run. I've got my own snowmobiles, and I'm taking these two out to Whitefeather's cabin."

Stephenson shrugged. "Suit yourselves. When you get done playing Hardy Boys, you can join us."

Carroway stood up. "Now we really have to leave."

"You can stay here if you want. You'll be a hell of a lot more comfortable, and I know you'll eat better. We even have extra new toothbrushes, and fresh jammies if you want. I mean, listen to the wind outside. You want to go back out in that?"

"Sounds like it's alive," Billy said. He turned to Sean. "Can we stay?"

Sean frowned. "I have to call Ottawa. And home."

Stephenson waved her hand. "You can use one of the satellite phones. We've got everything you need here. There's a recreation room in back, and it's got a bar. Let's go relax. Tomorrow's going to be a long day."

Sean looked at Carroway, who shrugged. "Guess we'll stay, then, if it's not putting you out."

Sean called Shepherd in Ottawa and gave his report. He was told to remain there and control the situation, which he knew was out of his hands at this point. He called home and spoke to Ree, assuring her that everything was fine.

They drank, played cards, and talked for hours as the storm thrashed around outside. Stephenson drank glass after glass of wine, watching the men with what seemed like predatory interest to Sean.

"I'm hungry for some entertainment," she said at last. "Carroway, what in the hell do you do up here all by yourself? Besides the obvious, that is?" She made a back-and forth motion with her wrist.

"I asked him the same question," said Billy.

"I mean, you're like Sergeant Preston and all, keeping the law up in this godforsaken wasteland, but what in hell brought you here?"

"I wanted to be alone after my wife died."

Stephenson actually seemed abashed for a moment. "Sorry. Guess I deserved that. But I'm surrounded by all this testosterone. How about something more than cards? How about a little arm wrestling? Any of you think you could take Russell here? Sean?"

"No thanks."

"What's the matter, afraid of a little competition?"

"No, I just don't want to be manly for your amusement."

"Party pooper. Billy would do it if I asked him, wouldn't you, Billy dear? Although it wouldn't be much of a contest."

"I'll do it," Carroway said. Sean looked at him, and Carroway winked.

"Bravo," said Stephenson. "A real man, at last. What say we put a little wager on it? Make it interesting?"

"What kind of wager?"

"Oh, say a hundred dollars that Russell wins."

"I'm on a pension. I don't have a hundred dollars."

"Hmmm," said Stephenson. "Then how about if you lose, Sean here has to kiss me."

"No way," said Sean, at the same time Carroway spoke. "Done."

Sean looked at Carroway, who nodded. "I got this."

"You damn well better have."

The table was cleared, and the opponents sat across from each other, right hands clasping their counterpart. Sean was looking at the size of Stephenson's bodyguard, and wondering how he was going to explain to Ree just how he had to pay off a debt.

Stephenson was standing over them, her eyes afire. Her hands wrapped around theirs. "Ready?"

Both men nodded.

"Go!"

Muscles bulging, the contest was on. Carroway was like a rock, unmoving, while Russell grunted and strained to put him down. They sat there gripped in struggle, neither gaining nor losing. Sean noticed a blue vein pulsing on the side of Russell's head.

A minute passed. Sean saw Russell blink furiously and thought he was crying, then realized it was only sweat running into the man's eyes.

Russell's forehead was furrowed, his eyebrows so close together they were almost touching. Carroway was intent, eyes narrowed, as he watched his opponent. Then slowly, inexorably, the tide turned against Russell. An inch of give, and then another, and the end came soon after, as Carroway pressed the bigger man's hand to the table.

Billy gave a whoop. Stephenson shrugged and went to a purse in the corner. She came back with a bill, and handed it to Carroway. The skin around her mouth looked tight. "You're a lot stronger than you look, old man."

Carroway waved the money as he went over to the bar, then slapped it down. "Looks like the drinks are on me, boys."

Everyone but Russell laughed.

Sean sidled up to Carroway, who was rubbing his chest. "You look a little gray. You okay?"

"Right as rain. I just proved who's the lead dog in the pack."

Sean toasted Carroway with a beer. "I thought I was going to have to do a lot of explaining when I got home."

Carroway had a shot-glass of whiskey before him, and held it up, gazing into the amber liquid. "Things aren't always as they seem up here."

"Guess the hell not."

"All right," Stephenson called out. "Which one of you sissies thinks he can outdrink me?"

"Here we go again," said Sean.

***

That night, Sean awoke in the room he shared with Billy and Carroway. He got up in the darkness, listening to the rumble of Carroway's snoring. All was still as he made his way down the dim, frigid hallway to the shared bathroom, and he felt as if he was creeping through a mausoleum.

When he came out, Stephenson stood before him in a short silk robe. In the reflection of the bathroom nightlight, her eyes were luminescent. "Well hey there," she said. "Fancy meeting you here."

"The master suite doesn't have its own bathroom?"

"Oh, it does. I came out for you." She licked her lips, and Sean knew what Red Riding Hood had felt like.

His voice came out hoarse. "See you in the morning."

"Oh, come on," her voice was a velvet caress. "You're not married yet."

"Very flattering offer, but I'm not like that."

"At least *see* what's being offered." Stephenson's robe slipped from her shoulders, and her naked body was a living Greek statue, taut and lovely. Her breasts swelled slightly, the nipples stiff. Before Sean could react, she took a step closer, and appeared to trip, pitching forward. He caught her, and she pressed against him. Her hair had the scent of spring flowers as it brushed his skin.

"I'm cold," she said, her hand on his bare chest, her touch electric. "Come warm me up."

Sean's mouth was dry, and as he felt the heat of her breath, he felt a stirring of desire. He took her shoulders and pushed her to arm's length.

"No."

"You want to. You're trembling, you want it so bad. Come on. We can go rough, or we can go easy. Any way you want, big man."

"I said no."

"I can make good things happen for you," she said. "You going to stay forever in that dreary little office in Ottawa, or do you want something bigger and better? A promotion, a chance to get out? Security work for movie stars, maybe? Whatever you want."

"Jesus Christ."

A door in the hallway opened to show a sleepy face peering out.

Stephenson stabbed a finger. "Get back inside and stay there." The face disappeared, the door whooshing closed.

She studied Sean for a moment, then stooped to pick up her robe, holding it in her hand. "My room's the last door on the left, if you change your mind. I'll leave it unlocked." She walked away, putting a little extra roll in her hips, and Sean was angry at himself for watching her and for his need.

CHAPTER 18

Sean walked through a land of fire, on snow that didn't melt. Flames rose and danced all around him, but parted to let him through. Sweat poured from his body, but his hands and face were cold.

Huge wolves skirted the pillars of flame and glowered at him. Their tongues lolled obscenely, and their malevolent gaze followed his movements. He moved faster, seeing a lighted church ahead. More wolves circled, keeping pace. He fired at several with a pistol, but to no effect. There were human bodies in the flames, and the wolves began to feed on them.

Sean was now in church, where a Christmas party was in progress. He asked several people if they had seen the wolves, and they told him they were going skiing. Sean then walked through a field, ready to ski, but saw the dead grass on the hill, and knew they couldn't ski there. He looked at the chair lift, where a white-haired old man sat wrapped in a blanket. The man spoke, trying to tell him something, but Sean couldn't hear over the music being played.

Sean awoke in the unfamiliar room, disoriented and apprehensive. His arms lay out of the sheets, chilled by the cold air of morning. He tried to recall the dream, but the images fled before his conscious mind.

Carroway's bed was empty. Billy was on an air mattress on the floor, and Sean poked to wake him as he went past. He soon went downstairs, where Carroway handed him a cup of coffee. Several of Stephenson's team were already discussing plans in the big room.

"Snow's stopped for now," Carroway said. "We'll get out to the cabin today, and the other murder site, which isn't far. Ever ride a snowmobile?"

"Not in a long time," replied Sean. "Hey, Billy."

Billy grunted a greeting. "This is like a journey into my past. Oatmeal, snowmobiles, sleeping bags... I haven't done this stuff since I was a kid."

"Well, you got the hat for it," Carroway said. "Suppose it gives everyone something to laugh at. Tell that guy in the kitchen what you want for breakfast. I tried to make some eggs, but she brought an honest-to-god chef, and he won't let me touch anything. Make sure to eat hearty, because we'll be out in the cold all day."

"Out in the damn uninhabited wilderness, you mean."

"It's not uninhabited. It's just sparsely populated."

When they finished their meal, Sean and Billy dressed for the outdoors and then joined Carroway. He pointed to the other vehicles. "This old girl fired right up, but they had to use jumper cables on two of those things."

"Who did all the shoveling and plowing?"

"Her crew. Say what you want, but she's got 'em trained."

They drove for a half hour to Carroway's place. Carroway put the plow blade down and made a path in the drive.

"Grab that shovel and get to work. There's another one inside the garage. We'll load up the snowmobiles and I'll make some lunch to take with us."

A few minutes later, they had the flatbed tow trailer attached to the ball hitch on the rear of the International.

"Okay," Carroway said, indicating a snowmobile. "Bring that first one on over."

They dragged one of the snowmobiles over to the trailer, lifted the back end up onto the flatbed, then hoisted the heavier front end up and on, sliding it back. They pushed it to the side, leaving room for another machine. Both Sean and Billy were breathing heavily.

Carroway chuckled. "Takes a little effort, doesn't it?"

They repeated the process with the second snowmobile, which had been taken down from the chain lift. Carroway tossed Sean a coil of rope.

"Tie 'em down so they don't slide around."

With Billy's help, Sean ran the ropes over and around the machines, securing both, while Carroway hooked up the wire for the tail lights on the trailer.

Carroway started the International and eased forward into the driveway. Sean closed the garage door and stepped on the handle to push the door down all the way. He joined the other two in the truck and they pulled away.

They drove until they came to a truck turnaround, where the snow had been pushed back and spread out to make a passage through the high snowbanks. Carroway parked and Sean and Billy untied and unloaded the snowmobiles.

Carroway put a knee on the seat of one of the snowmobiles and turned the ignition key. The engine sputtered to life. Carroway tilted the machine on its side until the track was out of the snow, and gunned the engine. It roared louder, the treaded track spitting snow. Carroway set it back down, and repeated the process with the other one.

Sean remembered the older models, which started by yanking on a pull cord, like starting an old lawnmower. You had to pull hard and all the way through. It was a test of strength, and sometimes will. You learned what made it go, what energy and power were. Now everything turned with a key, and though it was much easier, Sean thought a little something was lost in the process.

They let the engines run to warm them up, and Carroway loaded supplies into the rear compartments of each. One of the snowmobiles started to creep forward, until Carroway squeezed his thumb on the brake.

"Rarin' to go," he shouted over his shoulder. "All set? You two ride together."

Sean got on the other machine. "I think I remember how these go." But he knew Carroway could not hear.

Sean sat and Billy got on behind him. Billy reached around and cupped Sean's chest like a woman's breasts.

"Hey, big boy. Can I ride with you?"

Sean elbowed him, and Billy let go.

The engine throttle worked by rotating the handle. Sean twisted it down a notch, and the snowmobile lurched ahead, catching Sean off balance. He settled in and gave it the gas, and the machine moved forward, the bottom track rolling along the snow.

Sean felt the wind sting his face, and stopped for a moment to pull down the mask part of his ski cap.

Carroway rode ahead, cutting a path through the fresh snow that made a track for Sean and Billy to follow. They navigated along a corridor through the underbrush, just barely wide enough for them to pass. Branches slapped at Sean from the side, and often dumped snow on him. He sometimes had to duck his head to avoid low-hanging limbs, and remembered to ride far enough behind Carroway to avoid bushes whipping back into him.

The movements came back to him through time, the shifting on the seat for balance around curves, and how to move. He was reminded of the fun he used to have, and began to enjoy the ride.

Sean was amazed at how crisp and beautiful everything looked. The complete lack of buildings was a refreshing change from Ottawa, and he continually turned to look at something new and wonderful. The hum of the powerful machine beneath him was intoxicating.

They rode past white-clad trees and over frozen streams. Sean had not been this close to nature in a long time, and he exulted in the contact. The land was seductive and alluring, with a chill beauty. There were no animals to be seen, only the thick white blanket that covered all.

Some time later, Carroway stopped and switched off his engine, and Sean pulled up and followed suit. Sean noticed his ears were still buzzing from the constant whine of the engine. He slipped off a glove and rubbed his face and ears with a bare hand. Everything seemed to be holding up to the cold well. Billy got off to stand in the snow, stretching, and Sean did the same.

Carroway handed each a steaming plastic cup of coffee. Sean cradled his in his hands, letting the vapor rise up to his face. He sipped, grateful for the warmth. Gazing around at the still whiteness of everything made him feel as if he had gone back in time to some ancient, primeval world. Hearing a cracking from within the trees, he wondered if it was the weight of snow snapping a branch, or if something alive was moving through the woods.

Warm from the coffee and refreshed from the break, Sean started his engine when Carroway did, and once more followed in his wake. Sean found he could let his mind wander, and turned his thoughts to Ree. She wouldn't enjoy it out here, for she liked having people around. He had been an only child, and so preferred solitude.

Time had little meaning out here. The sky had gone a duller gray, giving a depressing tinge to the landscape. The land took on an appalling sameness after miles of trees and snow. Sean was glad when they stopped for lunch.

Carroway took sandwiches out of the rear compartment and handed them out. He poured more coffee from the Thermos jug, and Sean removed his glove to take his. With both hands full, Sean made short work of the meal.

Billy had finished and was looking around. "So if we have to take a leak, we just hang it out alongside the trail here, or is it better to just pee down our leg?"

Carroway looked at him and shook his head.

Sean, too, realized that the earlier coffee was pressing on his bladder. He clumsily took a few steps off the trail to relieve himself, and discovered just how difficult the operation could be when fully dressed for winter. He was thoroughly chilled by the time he rearranged the layers, and got back to the snowmobiles.

Half an hour later, Carroway stopped his machine at the base of a hill, searching the terrain. He looked at the trees and back again, but shook his head. Sean followed him to the top of the hill and switched off his machine.

"The fight took place down there," Carroway pointed down the hill. "But the snow's covered it all. There's nothing left to see."

They went to the cabin of Jimmy Whitefeather, now a blackened ruin frosted with snow. Sean found a branch of dead wood, and used it to poke through the remains. He found nothing but charred stumps. He grunted, thinking how important fire was up here. He thought of the Jack London story, 'To Build a Fire,' and how the character's failure to get one going meant his death. He thought it ironic, in light of what happened up here.

The Crees had done an efficient job. Sean didn't believe there had been any spirits, but he was still spooked at the thought of the two dead people and their killer eating their flesh. He walked all around the site, just to be thorough.

"What do you think?" Billy looked at him.

Sean shrugged. "What can we do? The cabin's gone, the snow's covered the crime site, the killer's dead. No use in a crime lab."

"What about Whitefeather?"

"Walking Cloud said Whitefeather had lived on the Reserve all his life, and had only left it once to go to the city. Hated it. He married his wife seven years ago, and there were no children."

"Think he just got cabin fever? Went crazy?"

"Who's to say?"

"What do we do about Walking Cloud? Cart him off to prison to die?"

"What's the point?" Sean looked around. "Look at this place, like a gulag for exiles."

"Doesn't seem to be anything left," Billy said, kicking at a black lump.

"We came all this way," Carroway said. "So I'll take you to the site where the father was killed. It's close by. But probably not much to see there, either."

Sean looked back at the place once more. The darkness of the ruin matched his mood. Three people dead, and all he had was the legend of a malevolent spirit. Ottawa liked things that were concrete, explainable. Sean and Billy got back on their machine and followed Carroway's snowmobile down the hill.

Several minutes later, Carroway stopped by a ruined stump, with the severed, snow-covered tree alongside. There had been no Christmas tree at the Reserve this year, and probably would never be again.

Sean found a corner of the smashed toboggan sticking up out of the snow. He picked it up and studied it, trying to will it to tell him something, give him some bit of information on what had happened. Sean thought of how in detective fiction the clever investigator could deduce the entire chain of events from a bit of cigar ash or a swatch of ripped fabric. He dropped the frayed wood, feeling frustrated.

Sean looked at the mutilated stump of tree, and thought of the custom of killing a thing to celebrate a birth. It made him think of the Druids, the ancient keepers of sacred groves. They would not have approved.

Other than the toboggan piece and the hacked tree, there were no signs of struggle. The snow had covered all tracks, even those of the Crees who came to the too-late rescue. It was just another ghost place where someone had died. No clues, only stories from the past. Sean looked up at Carroway.

"Seen enough?" Carroway said. His expression was unreadable.

"Not like there's much to see."

"But now you can say you have, though. Covered all the bases, checked everything out, just like in the manual."

"Yeah," Sean replied. "A real textbook case."

"Maybe we should take in the toboggan piece as evidence," Billy said. "Then we at least have something."

"Leave it," said Sean.

They left the place of death behind and moved off into the forest. Carroway weaved through the trees, taking them on a shortcut, which eventually led them back to the trail they had taken in. Riding was easier on the already broken-in trail.

The sky was already tinged with the end of the day, growing dimmer as light ran from the sky. There was no real sunset, just a sudden dark as everything went to black.

Their headlights bobbed through the gloom in a surreal way, which to Sean made the landscape suddenly eerie and menacing. The red taillight of Carroway's machine winked obscenely from up ahead. The wan headlight showed tree branches turned into skeletal fingers.

Sean was spooked when he saw yellow eyes watching them from the woods. He did not relax until they reached Carroway's vehicle. Sean groaned as they loaded the machines onto the trailer, now realizing how tired he was.

Carroway held the door open for a second before he got in, sniffing the air.

"What is it?"

"Gonna snow again."

CHAPTER 19

Sean hobbled out to the kitchen and drank coffee while Carroway made breakfast.

"How you feeling?"

"Pretty stiff," Sean admitted. "Got quite a workout yesterday."

"You gonna be okay to do it again today? We'll hook up with the crazy lady and her team."

"Sure, I'm supposed to keep an eye on her, and I've investigated everything else that I think I can. Did I miss anything?"

"No, just your open-and-shut case of cannibalism. What do you think Ottawa will do?"

"Probably nothing, as anything else would require a trial, and press, and everything else. If word doesn't leak out, they may be content to forget about this."

Billy came in, took some coffee, and slowly eased into a chair, grimacing. "I can't move. Think I sprained something yesterday."

"You serious?"

"And I can't take that cold. I never played hockey, like you, so I never got that used to it."

"You have to adapt."

"I hate to say this, fellas, but there's no way I can do that again today. Can you drop me off at Lorna's?"

Carroway looked at him. "Are you really going to chicken out on us?"

"What's the big deal? I'm just dead weight on the back of the machine. Admit it, you guys can move faster without me."

Sean shrugged. "It's true."

"Hey, are we going to be home in time for New Year's Eve? I've got a party to go to."

Sean smacked his head. "That's right. Day after tomorrow. Maybe Stephenson can find her Wendigo today and we can go home."

Carroway snorted. "Damn waste of gasoline, if you ask me."

"I don't know how long Ottawa's going to want us out here, tooling around the countryside. She might never leave."

"Then I guess something big better happen today, if you boys want to get home for your holiday."

They went through their morning business, dressed and went out to the garage. They were soon on their way, under a gray sky that for the moment was not dropping any more snow. Carroway kept glancing up, however, and looked like he was calculating in his head.

They arrived at the hunting camp and went inside.

Stephenson greeted them. "Howdy, boys. Missed you yesterday."

"Find any Wendigos?" Carroway smiled at her.

"Want to bet that hundred I do find it?"

"Hell yes."

"Come here and I'll show you where we searched." She led the way over to the maps, and indicated a grayed out zone. "That's what we covered. We hope to do another section today."

"You better move fast," said Carroway. "More snow coming."

"Goddamnit." Stephenson raised her voice. "Miller! Are we supposed to get another storm?"

"Radar says it moved off."

"Well it looks like it's coming back." She chewed her lip. "How much time do we have?"

Carroway stroked his chin. "End of the day. Just get 'em back by supper."

"Good. That's enough time. I've got something for you boys." She went to a table and picked up some items, handing Sean a satellite phone and a small device.

"What's this?"

"A tracking device. In case you boys get lost, we can find you. All my teams have them." She clicked a button. "There. Now I know where you are at all times."

They went in a caravan of vehicles, and unloaded at the checkpoint. Once in the open, their snowmobiles sank in the new snow, and slowed to a lumbering pace. The trail through the brush was clear enough, and they traveled the track for several miles.

The air pressure dropped, and a wet, clinging snow came down. Sean's mind was fuzzy, as if with a hangover, and he rode on like an automaton, not truly paying attention. All he had done and not done in his life weighed upon him and pressed his mind to dullness as the engine droned on. He thought of the past year, and the one yet to come, but the unending snow-covered land and the weather blended everything into a gray fog in his mind.

Sean strayed from the track occasionally, then had to slog back slowly in the unbroken snow. He almost ran into Carroway, who had stopped. Sean lumbered a few steps away to urinate on a fir tree. The cold did a bit to bring him to his senses, but he was physically and mentally drained. His arms felt weighted in the heavy material of his layers of clothing and the snowsuit. The wool scarf had been dampened with either sweat or snow, and it bothered him with a maddening itch. He scrabbled at it, pulling it from him, and tucked it in the back compartment. The cold air felt good.

They took off again, Sean feeling sullen and logy, doing his best to keep the throttle open and not get too far behind.

The trees began to swim in his vision and hem him in. He gulped air, feeling restricted. Branches seemed alive, clutching at him greedily, and he fought his way through them as if they had been leprous beggars. Feeling claustrophobic, he unzipped his parka.

Sean missed a spot where Carroway had swerved to avoid a partially exposed fallen tree, and ran over it. The snowmobile bucked and overturned, pitching him into the snow. His head smacked into a tree.

Carroway came riding back, a look of concern on his face. He lumbered over through the drifts.

"You okay?"

"I'm not sure," Sean said. "What happened?"

"You hit that log. If you'd followed my track, you'd see where I went around it. Weren't you paying attention?"

"Guess not."

"You want to sit up now?"

"Sure," Sean replied. He rolled onto his right arm for leverage and struggled to a sitting position.

"No broken bones?"

"No. Hit my head, though."

"Let's have a look," Carroway said, stripping off his gloves. He eased the ski cap off Sean's head and exposed the wound high on the scalp by the hairline. There was a short, ugly cut over a swelling lump.

"Doesn't look pretty," Carroway said, inspecting Sean's pupils for signs of concussion. "How many fingers am I holding up?" He held up two digits on one hand and one on the other.

"Three. Can I get back on the ice, coach?"

"You're okay. Just sit still until I bandage that head."

Carroway came back with the first aid kit. He removed a sterile compress and tore open the package. He squeezed out a bit on antibiotic ointment onto the compress. Carefully and gently, he placed the compress on Sean's head.

"Hold that right there," Carroway said. Sean raised his hand and held the bandage until Carroway wrapped it with an Ace bandage, winding around Sean's head.

"You giving me a turban?"

"Quiet."

"Make sure I can get my ski cap back on."

"Yeah, yeah, hold still."

"Want me to tell your fortune?"

"Pipe down while I finish. There." Carroway handed Sean his cap, who slowly got it on without disturbing the bandage. They put their gloves on and Carroway helped Sean to his feet. They beat the snow from their clothes.

Sean looked at the overturned snowmobile, where the front skis seemed to wave to him like crippled legs. The two men worked to rock the machine back to upright. It took some effort, and Carroway was breathing heavily when they finished. He sat on the snowmobile seat, rubbing his chest. He seemed about to say something, before he checked himself and remained quiet. He brushed snow from the dials, and fiddled with the engine.

Sean touched his cap where the bandage was, aware of a throbbing ache in his head, starting behind the eyes. The pain was startling and severe, and he stumbled when he took a step. The wind picked up a handful of loose snow and playfully tossed it in Sean's face. He gasped in surprise, but the cold felt good.

Carroway started the injured machine, listened to it sputter and cough, and revved it while tipping it on its side. Sean saw the cracked windshield and pointed to it.

"Sorry," He shouted to be heard over the engine.

"Cheap plastic," Carroway said. "Don't worry about it."

Sean noticed that snow was falling around them. He looked up and tugged Carroway's sleeve like a little boy. Carroway looked up and frowned.

"Storm's blown right back. We'd better get going."

Sean nodded, but the movement caused a flash of pain. He decided not to move his head too much. He sat on the snowmobile and looked glumly at the broken windshield. He slowly put his hands on the steering bar. His hands looked unfamiliar, distant, but they responded to commands. He watched the snow collect on his gloves.

Carroway came up beside him. The sound of both engines pounded and echoed in Sean's head, but he gave a thumbs-up signal to Carroway and watched him accelerate away. Sean goosed his own machine, and moaned as the increased sound sharpened the pain he felt. His shoulder also sent its own message of agony, and Sean realized he must have wrenched it when he fell.

Sean followed Carroway's track, and Carroway circled back whenever Sean lagged behind, but each time Sean waved him on. Sean felt an overwhelming desire to sleep, just close his eyes and shut out everything. As the pain hammered in his head, the snow pounded at his face, refusing him rest or respite. He blinked and wiped his goggles with a swipe of the glove. He squinted to see Carroway ahead of him, and thought he saw things flickering at the edge of his vision.

Feeling the drowsiness take him, Sean leaned to scoop a handful of snow as he rode, and rubbed the snow into his face. The cold kept his awake for a few minutes, and when it had worn off, he did it again.

Carroway was waiting at the fork of a trail when Sean arrived. Sean waved him on, and Carroway went to the right. Sean stopped for a moment, breathing deeply. He closed his eyes, feeling the pain, insistent and absorbing.

Sean opened his eyes and started down the track to the left. The snow seemed harder to plow through, and Sean wondered why the track was such hard going. He realized he wasn't following Carroway anymore, and panicked. He turned the machine around, the wind blasting in his face.

Back at the fork, Sean could not decide which was the correct path. He couldn't think through the pain, and took off blindly, hoping he was on the path. Over the roar of the engine, he thought he heard something up ahead. He drove on, punch-drunk but determined. He heard the sound again, off to his left. He turned the machine, but it bogged down in deep snow. He tried to tug it loose, but the pain was too much, and he switched the engine off instead. That made the pain lessen somewhat.

Sean began to move clumsily through the drifts, toward the sound. He concentrated on a small point in front of him, his head swirling like a maelstrom, pulling him to a dark center. His breath was ragged, the cold searing his lungs, but he was sweating with exertion. The wind drove harder, chilling him.

Sean hesitated, unsure of which way to go. He heard the sound again, a high, unearthly moan, carried on the wind. His head was pounding once more. He followed the sound, buffeted by the merciless wind.

Sean thought the trees moved, and wondered if he was hallucinating. Squinting into the wind, he saw one of the trees advance toward him. He laughed, thinking it was funny. He laughed harder when he saw that the tree was covered in fur and had a face. He laughed until the tree screamed, and Sean echoed the cry before slipping into the black unconscious silence he so desired.

PART III

CHAPTER 20

Billy opened the hospital room door to find Ree asleep in the garish and uncomfortable-looking chair next to Sean's hospital bed, a magazine open on her lap.

"Ree," he said.

She started, eyes blinking. The magazine slid onto the floor.

"I'm sorry," Billy began.

She stood up. "What the hell, Billy?"

"I—"

"What happened? What the hell happened up there?"

"He got lost, hit his head."

"How could he get *lost*? Where were you?"

"I wasn't with him, I was—"

"You're his goddamned *partner*. Why weren't you with him?"

"I couldn't take it," Billy cried out, tears in his eyes, anguish in his voice. "It was too goddamned cold, and I just couldn't take any more. Riding around the woods on those goddamned snowmobiles, chasing something that doesn't exist."

"What are you saying? You were investigating a murder."

"Yeah, well, there was some other shit going on."

Ree took a deep breath. "I think you better tell me everything."

A few minutes later, Billy finished telling her what had occurred up north.

Ree pinched her fingers on the bridge of her nose. "You're telling me that a bunch of grown people were off on a wild goose chase? And that's why Sean is like this? Look at him. *Look at him!*" Ree turned to the bed, where wires and tubes strung out from Sean's body like spiderwebs, giving him sustenance and connecting him to machines.

"I've been in this damn room for two days, waiting to see if he's going to regain consciousness. We should all be out partying for New Year's Eve, and instead I get to see him lay there with those tubes and wires sticking out of him like something out of a horror movie. We're supposed to get married, and now all I see is this. It scares me, Billy."

"It scares me too."

"I haven't even told my family, you know that? All the people I love, and I can't stand the thought of them down here smothering me. I'm all alone. All I can do is pray and cry, and I've been doing a lot of both."

"He'll be okay. He wasn't out there that long, and the X-rays—"

"He was excited to be going up there. He wanted to get out. He said it wasn't dangerous."

"It wasn't supposed to be. It was just an accident."

"Because you idiots were chasing some goddamned legend. That doctor you spoke of. It's her fault, isn't it? If I ever get my hands on that bitch, I'll kill her."

"It was her tracking device that let them find him. She saved his life. And she paid to have him med-evaced out and flown here."

"Oh, yes, and she paid for these lovely dead flowers, too. How nice. I'll be sure to thank her after I kick her ass."

"Ree—"

"Stop talking, Billy. I'm pretty angry at you. I'm angry at all of you, even Sean, and I'm guilty about that, too. You can stay, but just don't say anything, okay?"

Billy nodded, and sat in the other chair, an ugly twin to Ree's.

Ree went to Sean's side. She smiled and squeezed his hand. As she did, she thought she saw his eyelids flutter. Sucking in her breath, hardly daring to hope, she tightened her grip on his hand, as Sean opened his eyes.

Ree cried and touched Sean's face. She wanted to hug him, but was afraid of disturbing all the medical apparatus.

"Oh, Sean," she said, tears slipping down her face. "We were so afraid for you. Are you all right? They said you hit your head. You're in the hospital, back here in Ottawa."

Sean did not speak, and Ree looked closely at him, realizing something was wrong. His eyes were hard and glittering, and she could see nothing but black. He looked at her with an unreadable expression, and she saw nothing of Sean in those eyes. Her breath hitched.

"Billy, go and get the nurse," she said, her voice too high. "And get the doctor in here. Quick."

Billy ran.

Ree tried to pull away, but Sean clung tightly. He pulled her hand close to his face, and she thought for a moment he was going to kiss it. Instead, he moved his other arm, IV and all, and grasped her arm with both his hands. Ree was puzzled, but didn't resist.

Sean pulled her arm to his mouth. She couldn't believe what he was doing, and yanked her arm away an instant before he bit into it. His teeth snapped together on air instead of flesh.

He gave a hard jerk. The side rails of the bed were down, and she was pulled off balance, falling on top of him. The IV stand toppled, crashing to the floor. Ree screamed. She tried to regain her balance, but Sean grabbed her hair.

Ree remembered the self-defense he'd taught her. She cocked her free hand back at the wrist, curled her fingers down, and drove the heel of the hand up into Sean's chin. His grip on her hair loosened. She tried to roll away, but he held on with one hand and clubbed her with his other arm. She covered up and took the blows on her forearms, still screaming.

Suddenly there were other arms reaching across her. She was released, and she rolled off and sank to the floor, as the room filled with people. She sat with her head against the bed and began to sob.

CHAPTER 21

Ree was waiting in the back of a coffee-shop, not far from the building where Sean worked.

"Mr. Shepherd," Ree rose. She had met him only once, and thought him a little too stiff and formal, too 'military' for her taste. Sean might have had respect for him, but today the man was her adversary.

"Miss Tourneau. Let me express my deepest regret for this unfortunate occurrence." Shepherd looked sympathetic and sounded genuinely concerned. Perhaps he was, but Ree wanted his aid, not his sympathy. "How are you holding up?"

"Not very well, I'm afraid." She looked directly at him. He did not blink or try to evade her gaze.

"Yes, I can well imagine. Shall we sit?"

Ree nodded and did so. "What I would like," Ree began. "Is to know what happened to turn my fiancé into a monster. He tried to hurt me, he's under restraint in a place where I can't see him, and he hasn't spoken anything resembling human speech. Oh, and he snarls like an animal, and tries to bite people. And you people told me it was a snowmobile accident."

Ree had tried to keep the anger and bitterness out of her voice, but failed. She fought for control, to keep back the stinging tears that would mean her defeat in this game. Shepherd wouldn't deal with a hysterical woman. He would respect control. She forced herself to appear calm.

"What did he tell you about the case?"

"Nothing. Only that there was a murder."

"Yes." Shepherd said, and Ree knew he was sizing her up, figuring how much to tell her. "A Cree native killed his wife and another man, and cannibalized their bodies."

Ree sat impassive, her expression stony. No wonder Sean hadn't told her.

Shepherd went on. "His people burned him, and we sent Sean up there to find out why."

"And what did he find out?"

"It's very odd…" Shepherd hesitated.

"I promise I won't run to the press, if that's what you're worried about. At least if you're honest with me. But I need to know."

"Of course," Shepherd agreed. "The people there believe in a spirit— a demon, if you will— and they believe the murders were caused by this demon spirit."

Ree drew in her breath as a flash of anger surged through her. "You're telling me Sean was out hunting a ghost?" Billy had told her the truth.

"We don't believe in ghosts."

"Then what do you believe?"

Shepherd looked down. "His mental state is the reported condition of those possessed by this spirit."

"You think he's *possessed*?" Ree's grip on the arm of the chair was murderous.

"It's possible that *he* does. We don't know, and for that, I'm sorry. There was no trace of hallucinogenic drugs in his system. What's going on in his mind is a complete mystery."

"And no way of knowing how long he'll be like this."

"We've had two of the best specialists in the country examining him. They're as puzzled as we are. He has no prior behavioral clues pointing to anything like this. No one can accurately predict what will happen."

Ree turned her head away for a moment. It was all she allowed herself. "Was he part of some government experiment?"

Shepherd looked her full in the face. "No. I swear to you, this was not something we did."

"He went to see someone in Montreal before he went up. Someone involved in this mess."

"Yes." Shepherd sat watching.

"I would like to speak with whoever that was. They might be able to tell me something."

"We've already retraced his steps. We haven't found anything—"

"You don't know him," Ree cut in. "I do. I know how his mind works. This just didn't happen out of the blue. A bump on the head didn't turn him into what he is now. Something else went on, something he did or saw. I'm going to find out what that was."

Shepherd leaned back in his chair. He looked at Ree so hard she felt he could read her mind. She returned the gaze, steady and unswerving. Shepherd nodded, almost imperceptibly, accepting the strength of her will over his need to refuse.

"Ordinarily I couldn't allow it. But then, there's nothing ordinary about all this. You're already in deeper than you should be, but there's nothing we can do about that. I could tell you it would do no good, but you wouldn't accept it. You're a fighter, just like him."

Shepherd smiled, ever so slightly, and Ree appreciated it for the rarity she knew it to be. She nodded, accepting the compliment.

"That's why I know he'll make it," Shepherd went on. "He's young and strong, and he has you."

Shepherd took out a business card and wrote on it. He handed the card to Ree.

"There's his number and address in Montreal. I don't know how much help he'll be, but I wish you luck."

Ree glanced at the card before putting it in her purse. "And that woman doctor. The one who found him. I want to speak with her as well."

"She's not with us."

"I don't care. I want her contact information."

Shepherd made a slight nod. "We can get that for you."

"And that man they stayed with up north. He might know something."

"That could be difficult. He's not an easy man to get in touch with."

"Difficulties can be overcome when the need is great."

"So they can. All right, we'll see what we can do to arrange that."

"One more thing."

Shepherd raised an eyebrow.

"I want to see him again."

"Of course. It's a security facility, with restrictions. I'll have Billy take you."

Shepherd stood, and shook her hand before leaving. After he had gone, she let her breath out. She had been afraid he was going to stonewall her. She had done very well indeed.

CHAPTER 22

When Atherton opened the door, he was about what Ree had envisioned, looking like a professor at home. His hair was combed back, and his appearance brought to mind a word she had heard the nuns use back in school: natty. She smiled and held out her hand as she introduced herself.

"Dr. Atherton? I'm Gabrielle Tourneau."

"Won't you come in?"

Inside, he asked her to remove her boots, and he carefully hung up her coat.

They went to the living room, where a woman sat on the couch, smoking a cigarette. Atherton coughed and waved his hand.

"This is Doctor Lorna Stephenson."

Ree stiffened. "Why is she here?"

"I assumed you wanted to know what had happened up north."

Ree paused, and then put it together. "You brought her into this."

"Well, I—"

"I brought myself in," Stephenson said. "The good doctor here is a friend of mine, and when talk of the Wendigo came up, he naturally included me."

Ree looked at her. "I've seen you on TV. Pierre Burton interviewed you."

Stephenson nodded.

"Billy said you crashed the investigation, and they couldn't get rid of you."

"And how is our dear little Billy? Has a bit of a crush on me, I'm afraid."

Ree's initial mild dislike was cemented. "He's feeling guilty for what happened to my fiancé. I wonder if you are."

"Miss Tourneau— can I call you Gabby?"

"No," Ree snapped. "That's not my name."

"Well then. Miss Tourneau, what happened to Sean was very much *not* my fault."

"Really? Would they have been out chasing ghosts if you hadn't pushed them?"

"The Wendigo isn't a ghost. It's a living thing."

"And you insisted they go looking for it."

Stephenson shrugged. "We were doing it. Nobody forced them."

"I know Sean. If there was an investigation, he was probably told to keep an eye on things, and so had to watch you."

"Maybe so, but also realize that if it wasn't for me, he'd probably still be out there, covered in snow somewhere in the forest."

Ree took a step backward and touched her stomach.

"Are you all right?" Atherton looked concerned. "Can I get you anything?"

"Some coffee would be nice, thank you. Black."

"Right away." Atherton scurried off.

Stephenson took a puff from her cigarette. "How far along are you?"

"What?" Ree felt the blood rise to her face.

"You're pregnant, dear. How far along?"

"How did you know?"

"Women can tell. Men, they don't have a clue, but we know."

"A few weeks," Ree said.

"Sean didn't mention it. Ah, before the wedding. So you probably haven't told the families yet."

Ree blushed even more. What was this woman, who could read her so well?

"We won't tell the menfolk. It'll be our secret."

Bitch. Using a favor to gain Ree's trust. Ree's dislike kicked up another notch.

Atherton came back out. "It's brewing. Ready in a second. Please, have a seat."

Ree sat in the proffered chair. "Right now Sean's in a private institution, not allowed any visitors. I have to look at him through wire-mesh glass. He's like a wild animal, so he's heavily sedated and restrained."

Stephenson spoke. "Did he say anything before he tried to bite you?"

Ree shook her head, but wondered how the woman knew that as well. "No, he never spoke. Just animal grunts."

Atherton's eyes were focusing on Ree's. "What do you know about the Wendigo?"

"Only what Billy told me in the hospital. That's what Sean came to you to ask about. Because something terrible happened up north."

"Yes."

"Well, it seems like Sean was influenced somehow, and believes he is possessed by this Wendigo thing."

"Oh, my, this is exciting. I've studied this for years, but never dreamed of having an actual case—"

"I'm so very glad we could accommodate you," Ree snapped.

"Oh, Miss Tourneau, I am so sorry. I really didn't mean that to come out the way it did."

"The coffee," said Stephenson.

"Oh, yes, I'll be right back."

Stephenson stubbed out her cigarette. "Forgive me for asking, but did he ever have any psychological problems before this?"

"No."

"No depression?"

Ree thought. "Well, a little blue sometimes, but—"

"Medications?"

Ree shook her head.

Atherton came back, and handed Ree a cup and saucer. She recognized the Limoges china, and wondered why a single man had something so delicate and fine. Ree imagined him calculating his book deal and scholarly papers.

"How do we get him back to normal?"

"Well. Most likely a long period of psychoanalysis and therapy."

"Fuck that," said Stephenson. "We need an exorcism."

"What?"

"We could perform an exorcism rite. Or more accurately, have the Crees do it. They have ceremonies for this kind of thing."

"Are you kidding me?" Ree thought about throwing her coffee at the woman.

"Hear me out. It doesn't matter if *we* believe in it, as long as *Sean* does. Do you see what I mean? The process of going through that convinces his subconscious that he's cured. If belief got him into this state, it can get him out."

"How would you go about it?"

"It has to be real, the true ceremony. We'd need the cooperation of the Crees, the people who believe it themselves."

Ree thought for a minute, overcoming her revulsion at what she was considering. As a devout Catholic, this ran against everything she believed. "Would they do it?"

Atherton jumped in, barely able to contain himself. "Possibly."

"What exactly is involved in this ceremony?"

"It's very arduous. A great deal of heat is involved, to drive out the spirit. There's the mental stress, of course, but he's young and strong, so he should be all right. But it may not work. There is no way to tell."

"But it has a chance?"

Stephenson shrugged. "If someone has a better plan, now would be the time to speak up."

They were silent.

"Okay, then," said Stephenson. "You won't like this at all, but you're going to need my help."

CHAPTER 23

"A chandelier?" Ree stared at it. "What kind of idiot hauls a chandelier up this far to put in a goddamn hunting camp?"

"Same kind who has to slice the heads off animals and stick them on a wall," Stephenson said, gesturing.

"What the hell is wrong with men?"

"Where do you want to start?" Stephenson snorted. "Billy, why don't you take her upstairs and give her that last room on the right? And get her bags for her, be a dear. You and Carroway take the room you had last time."

Billy took Ree up the staircase. "Everyone here is sorry for the mess, Ree, and we'll all do what we can. What happened to Sean hit Pete pretty hard. He looks like he's aged ten years in the last week."

Ree was about to say that Sean looked even worse, but held her tongue.

Billy went on. "I know the church still does exorcisms, and even though there sure as hell isn't any church out here, it's still pretty weird, you know?"

When they had all gathered back downstairs, Stephenson laid out the battle plan. "The Crees have agreed to the ceremony, so we'll be there first thing tomorrow morning.

Anybody who isn't one hundred percent on this better not go with us. Anybody makes a crack about the legitimacy of the thing is going to find themselves walking back to civilization. Are we completely clear on that?"

She gave assignments and set them all to their tasks. She approached Ree. "I know it's not likely, but try to get some rest tonight. We don't know how long it's going to take."

Ree swallowed. "I want to say thank you for what you're doing for Sean. I know this has cost you, not just money, but time and resources. We appreciate it."

Stephenson looked at her with an unreadable expression. "You two are very lucky to have each other."

"And we're lucky you came along. The government was not so helpful."

"Honey, they want this all swept under the rug. Why do you think they sent your man and Billy? A couple of junior investigators who'd do what they were told. They'd just as soon this would all go away."

"Why didn't you bring Atherton? Couldn't he have helped?"

"That dimwit doesn't believe in the Wendigo. He's a bit like my father. Thinks it's just a mass hallucination caused by psychological factors. Of course there's no demon involvement, no real cannibalism 'infection,' it's just that people see this thing and freak out. But he doesn't buy the existence of a physical creature. So I told him he couldn't come. He actually cried. I'll invite him to the party when we bring it back, though, get a good look at his face."

***

The morning was a whirl of activity as the team got packed into a half-dozen vehicles and made their way to the Reserve.

When they parked in the clearing, the Crees came out of the buildings. Carroway noticed the young Cree he had seen before, still scowling. The faces of the others were hard to read, but did not look hostile. Some hung back and looked afraid.

Walking Cloud came slowly out of the main hall, wrapped in a huge thick coat. He looked through the back window of the vehicle, at the bundled and still-sedated Sean.

Carroway made introductions. Several Crees removed Sean from the back of the vehicle and took the stretcher down the trail past the buildings. Everyone else fell in behind with Walking Cloud.

One of the Cree women tapped Ree on the shoulder. She smiled nervously, and held out her hand. Ree put out her own, and the woman pressed something into it, closed her eyes and murmured a prayer, before giving a final squeeze and walking away.

Ree looked at the object in her hand, a trinket made of bone and feather. She showed the object to the others.

"Looks like some kind of charm," Carroway said. "It shows they're on your side. They want the ceremony to work, not just for their sake, but for yours as well."

They came to a small shack half-buried in snow, and the men took Sean inside. Walking Cloud put up a hand to keep the outsiders from entering and said something in French.

"What did he say?" Carroway asked.

"He said we couldn't come in," Stephenson replied. "It's a sacred lodge, with a ceremony for them alone."

Ree started talking rapidly in French, her voice rising, but Walking Cloud remained impassive. He retreated into the shack and closed the door, shutting out the outsiders.

"Damn them and their patriarchy," Ree glared at the door.

"Don't think you'd want to be in there anyway," Stephenson said. "It's a sweat lodge, pretty intense. A dark, cramped space with a bunch of smelly, naked men."

"Sounds like the parties back at University," said Ree, trying to break the tension. It worked, and they had a laugh.

"Looks like it's going to be awhile," Stephenson said. "I sure wish they'd let Chuck film it."

Ree remembered a time when she was eight years old, and her parents had taken her dog to the veterinarian. All the grownups had assured her the animal would get better if they took it to the doctor. She had waited in the stuffy little room until the vet came out and told her that her beloved companion had gone to doggie heaven. She had screamed and cried bitterly over the loss, and over the betrayal. She had been lied to, and would never forget that, and never again trust grownups.

Now here she was again, in the waiting room, to see what would be done. She had to trust others to do the right thing. She would not allow herself to think of what would happen if this failed.

They trooped back to the community building, where Stephenson had her people bring in a new television set, a donation to the tribe. The Crees filled the hall to watch the color screen, though it still only got one channel. The group of outsiders sat apart, mostly lost in their own thoughts.

When Ree left to use the bathroom, Carroway spoke up. "I didn't want to say anything while she was here, but what do we do if this doesn't work? Will the Crees just turn Sean back to us and wish us luck?"

Stephenson replied. "They'll probably assume the Wendigo has control over him and want to burn it out. I don't want to have to use force, but there's not going to be any barbecue. We've got some rifles in the vehicles, and a pistol or two."

"Might want to let your people know that they may need to move fast."

"Thank you, Mister Carroway, for telling me the obvious. I brought weapons along for just such a contingency."

"Do you always talk down to people?"

"Yes. It saves time on explanations. Then I can think without all the chatter."

Ree came back in. "What are you talking about?"

"Mister Carroway and I were just arguing to pass the time," said Stephenson. "He thinks I'm an evil bitch, and I think he's a silly old man."

Carroway turned to Billy. "I'm starting to like her."

CHAPTER 24

All darkness, cold and silent. Hunger, a terrible, sharp-toothed animal gnawing from inside. From somewhere, a sensation of approaching heat. And sound. Chanting, growing ever stronger.

A horrible odor, then a feeling of something hot on the chest. Arms couldn't move to brush it away. Searing, driving out all other thoughts.

Dim light, heat, noise, smell. Going on and on. Too much, too much.

The morning had turned into afternoon, and still there was no news. They'd picked at the lunch Stephenson had brought in. The long afternoon wore on, interminable hours of dread and boredom.

It seemed as if time had stopped before the door opened and Russell came in. He bent to whisper in Stephenson's ear.

"What is it?" said Ree. "What happened?"

"He says it may have worked," Stephenson said. "There was a loud last scream that Walking Cloud says was the Wendigo leaving his body. They'll know for sure when he wakes up."

Several other Crees came in, men from the ceremony. They looked tired and drained. They waved off questions with a shrug. Time would tell, but they could not see him yet.

Two hours later, a messenger came to tell them that Sean had awoken. They bundled into their coats and boots, and picked up flashlights.

Carroway spoke to Stephenson. "Your men ready, just in case?"

"In case of what?" Ree grabbed Carroway's forearm.

"In case it didn't work," Stephenson said. "The Crees might think it's necessary to burn Sean, to drive the Wendigo from him. But that's not going to happen."

Ree made a sound in her throat. Stephenson looked at her. "Oh, did I steal your line? Sorry."

"Take it easy on her," said Carroway. "This is hard enough."

"She's a lot tougher than you think. But I guess we'll see just how tough in about five minutes."

They walked to the lodge, bobbing flashlight beams cutting slashes through the dark. Ree ran ahead, and was the first one in.

Sean's eyes opened. "Ree?" The voice was soft, barely audible. Ree cried out and was on her knees beside him. Sean's eyes were wide open now, and they were his own.

"Where am I?"

Walking Cloud came over and held Sean's face in his hands and gazed intently at him. The wrinkled corners of his mouth turned up, and he nodded to the others.

Ree flushed with joy, and Carroway let out a whoop. Ree gave Sean an awkward hug before realizing that he probably couldn't breathe with her weight pressed upon him.

CHAPTER 25

Ree paused before opening the apartment door, summoning her strength. The apartment was dark. Had Sean had gone out? Her heart thudded, possibilities tearing through her mind. Had Sean really been cured, or was he lying in wait? She stood framed in the doorway, afraid to enter her own home.

"Sean?"

"I'm here," a voice drifted in from the dark.

"I'm going to turn the light on, okay?"

"Sure."

She groped for the wall switch and flicked it up. Sean sat in a chair by the window, blinking and squinting. He wore the same sweat pants and T-shirt he had on when Ree had left for work that morning. She sniffed. He was unshaven, and apparently hadn't showered.

"You okay?" Her voice was soft.

"Yeah."

"Whatcha doing?" Keep it light and casual, she told herself.

"Just thinking." Sean was still looking out the window. There was a long pause. Ree bit her lip.

"Want spaghetti tonight? I'll make it special, the way you like it."

"Whatever."

She said nothing, not trusting herself to speak. Please, not another argument. She changed clothes and came out of the bedroom. Sean had not moved. She looked at the back of his head for a moment, an ache building in her. Eyes eyes stinging with hot tears, she went to the kitchen. She would make dinner, concentrate on that.

Ree looked at the wine rack for a long moment, but touched her stomach. With the baby coming, she'd have to deny herself. Sean wasn't drunk, either, for a change. At least not yet.

She set all her focus on making a meal. When all was ready, she called to the other room. Sean shuffled to the table, stooped and drawn like a beaten dog. She breathed deeply, pushing the anger away. Sean took few listless bites.

"How is it?"

"Fine," he mumbled, eyes down. His voice was so low she could hardly hear him.

"Want a beer?"

"No thanks."

"Well that's a switch," she snapped, ferociously stabbing a meatball. "I don't know whether to pity you, or get angry."

His gaze flicked up and met hers for a brief moment, before it shied away.

"Sorry," she said.

"Mmmhh," he grunted. They pushed the food around on their plates for a time.

Don't cry, Ree told herself. "Want to get out? Go see a movie?"

"Not tonight," he said, not even looking up.

"When, then?" Ree slammed her fork down on the table. "Tomorrow? Next week? Or maybe never. You've been back three weeks, and haven't left this place."

"I don't want to fight."

"Too bad!" Ree snarled. "I want *some* kind of reaction from you. I'm tired of walking on eggshells, afraid to say anything. At least when we fight, you're not a damn zombie. You haven't been alive since you got back, and I can't take it, I just can't."

Sean looked at her tears, hurt and helpless. He tried to form words that would comfort her, but nothing came out. Ree got up and went to the bedroom.

A few minutes later, Ree was surprised to see Sean come in. She dabbed at her eyes with a tissue.

"I have to go back," Sean said.

"Back? Why?"

"Whatever they did took away a part of me." He scuffed his feet on the rug. "Don't worry," was all he could offer. "I'll be all right."

"That's what you said the last time."

"I don't want to return there, but I have to. We can't go on like this."

"What's up there that you can get back?"

"I'm going to find that thing. The Wendigo."

"What are you talking about? It's some stupid legend, a spirit, a ghost."

"No, it's real. I saw it."

"Jesus, Sean, you can't be serious."

"That's why it freaked me out, made me the way I was. I didn't believe in it before."

"You haven't recovered. I'll call Shepherd in the morning."

"I don't need another psychiatrist," he snapped. "I need to find that thing."

"You imagined it. When you hit your head—"

"It was *real*, Ree, I saw it. I see it in my dreams. I've got some kind of connection that won't go away."

"My Tante Louise talks to the ghost of her dead husband. She thinks he's real."

"This isn't a ghost. But it will be after I find it."

"I don't want you going back up there. What about our baby?"

"I have to go. Look, I know what I'm up against now. I'll be ready this time."

"Ready for what? Ready to die?"

"No. To kill."

CHAPTER 26

"You look like hell," Carroway said, as Sean shook his hand.

"So do you."

Carroway chuckled. "Lost weight, too."

"And you as well."

Billy piped up. "Should we call it the Wendigo all-protein diet?"

Carroway shook his head. "You had to bring him?"

"I wasn't there for him before," Billy said. "I'll be there this time."

"Billy-boy," said Carroway. "I think that's the first time I've ever seen you dead serious."

"Like me better that way?"

"No, just stay a pain in the ass like you usually are."

"Great to see you too, Pete. Besides, we had to come back for more of that oatmeal."

They grinned at each other, and all was well.

Carroway looked at Sean. "I wanted to say—"

"Pete, it's all right. You didn't let me down, and Billy didn't either. It wasn't anybody's fault. I got lost."

"Well, stay close this time. Though I don't know why you'd want to come back."

"I see a ghost in my dreams, a black, smoking corpse. I guess it's Jimmy Whitefeather. It points at me, then turns and walks away, leaving oversized footprints in the snow. I don't know if he's seeking retribution from the tribe, and pointing to me because of a lack of meted-out justice, or because he wants the Wendigo killed, and points to me as the one to do it."

"What happens if you find what you're looking for?"

"We kill it."

A cloud passed across Carroway's face. "Kill the dragon, save the village, and everyone's happy, right? That about it?"

"As far as the government is concerned, this thing doesn't even exist. I'm on official leave. I guess Ottawa hopes that by running around in the woods out here, I'll either be cured, or at least stop being a problem. But I ran into something out there, even though the only ones that believe it are Stephenson, me, and the Crees."

"You're sure about that?"

"Yeah, I didn't just go crazy. I lost a part of me, though, and I have to get it back. So I have to find that damn thing."

"Are you sure you're not just looking for revenge?"

"It's more than that. I guess our fates are intertwined somehow."

"Jesus, you sure got metaphysical."

"Dying will do that for you."

Carroway looked embarrassed. "Well, get in and I'll take you to the camp. You too, sidekick."

Billy frowned. "Hey, even the Lone Ranger needed a sidekick."

Sean smiled. "Yeah, someone has to get the luggage, right Tonto?"

"Kemo Sabe can kiss my ass."

"Hey, don't be that way. What does Kemo Sabe mean, anyway?"

"Means damn fool in a white hat who's going to get us both killed someday."

***

When they walked through the door of the hunting lodge, Stephenson put out her cigarette and came over to hug Sean.

"Welcome back, you big dumb lug. You don't have to go all freaky frozen stiff. I know this is as close as I'm going to get. Your Ree is rather protective."

Sean relaxed a little. "Thank you for everything you did. How's the search going?"

"Does the fact I look like shit tell you anything? There's a reason these goddamned things haven't been found yet. Too damn clever by half. We search every day we can, but there's a storm twice a week. I just don't know."

"I found it once," said Sean. "I can find it again."

"From your mouth to God's ear," said Stephenson, eyeing him. "Guess I'm not the only one who looks like shit. You sure you're okay to be out all day?"

"Physically and mentally."

"Good. Russell's out leading the charge. You can join them when you're ready."

"I'll need a weapon."

"Take your pick," Stephenson gestured to a gun cabinet by the wall, now stocked with a variety of firearms. Sean chose an Armalite semi-automatic rifle, and took several clips of ammunition. "I'm going to go sight this in. Okay to shoot out back?"

"Nobody's off in that direction. You're good to go."

Carroway said. "I'll get my thirty-ought six and join you."

Billy selected a pump-action, twelve-gauge shotgun. "This could be fun."

Stephenson looked at them and shook her head. "Boys."

Half an hour later they came back in, red-faced from the weather.

Sean blew on his hands. "I'd forgotten how cold it is up here. It's like some great gray beast that's waits just past the firelight, waiting for the fire to die down a little, so it can rush in and devour us."

"My, but we wax poetic."

"My newfound eloquence."

Carroway looked as if he wanted to speak, but changed his mind.

"What is it?" Sean said.

"Your eyes don't focus on what's in front of you. They're always looking back over my shoulder, as if scanning for something. You've got the faraway vision. The Crees would say you've been touched by the gods."

"Touched a little too closely for my taste."

"Feel like you have any special powers?"

Billy grinned. "He can't fly, if that's what you mean. The X-ray vision isn't working too well, either."

Sean looked serious. "Sometimes I look down at my hands and I don't recognize them, like they belong to somebody else. Or I'm seeing through someone else's eyes. I start itching all over, and wonder if I'm in someone else's skin."

"Bet the doctors in Ottawa would love to hear that."

"Yeah, I didn't tell them everything. They'd have kept me locked up. So I smiled and said all the right things."

"Did you tell Ree?"

"No."

"She knows something's wrong, though."

"Kind of hard for her not to." Sean sighed.

"But you're telling me."

"We're all in this together. And you still feel guilty."

"Well, dammit, I—"

"Answer me this, then. If it was the other way around, and it had been you instead of me, would you be blaming me?"

"I guess not."

"So afford me the same respect, then."

Carroway looked thoughtful. "You think it was meant to happen? Fate, then?"

"Maybe something like that."

"Ah, you've gone completely loony. I've been years here and only gone a little crazy. You come for one week and you're off to commune with the spirits."

"I'd rather commune with some lunch."

CHAPTER 27

Exhaust fumes from the vehicles curled and danced in the frozen air. Sean realized he'd become more vulnerable to the cold now, feeling it as a menacing presence, slyly worming its way through his clothing to attack his skin. He shivered, and wondered if by driving out the Wendigo from him, they had driven out his tolerance for cold as well. He zipped the parka up all the way to the top, and wound the scarf tighter around his neck, preferring the itch to the cold.

Sean watched Carroway, and noticed the older man moving more slowly and deliberately. It was the way Sean himself had moved after his recovery, with the discovery of fragility, of weakness that heralded mortality. Sean was saddened at the loss of Carroway's vitality, and realized that others beside himself had suffered.

"Look at us," Sean shook his head. "Some monster hunters."

"Maybe we'll be lucky," Billy said. "And the Wendigo will be on crutches."

"Why would he be on crutches, Billy?"

"Maybe he had a skiing accident."

They drove to the rally point in silence, as if to a funeral. The snowbanks formed a corridor, channeling them to their destination. To Sean, it was a tunnel from which he could not escape. He felt like Theseus, blindly stumbling through the dark Maze, listening for the heavy breathing of the Minotaur. He was shuttling between the worlds again, and the boundaries were slipping.

To kill the Wendigo, Sean had to keep thinking of it as a monster, although it was a creature just trying to live. But it had committed the unpardonable sin of being dangerous to Man, and it must be mastered, killed, for Man's peace of mind.

When they got to the rally point, Carroway came to a stop and shut off the engine. They sat there for a moment, loathe to leave the warmth and comfort of the vehicle.

"Let's get rolling."

Stephenson came up to them when they got out. "Each one of you wear one of these tracking devices. No one gets separated."

"What kind of idiot would do something like that?" Billy grinned at Sean, who ignored him.

"It's going to snow," said Sean.

Carroway looked up, cocked his head to the side. "He's right."

"Goddamnit," said Stephenson. "How long have we got?"

Sean shrugged. "Few hours. Time enough."

Stephenson nodded. "Okay. Sean, you can lead. But don't get too far ahead. Take this machine, though, it's quieter than those damn old ones. I don't want them making so much racket they scare the Wendigo off."

"No. Give me one of Carroway's. It's good that they're louder. All that noise hurts the head. Might make the Wendigo attack."

"So now you've got a mystical bond with this thing?" Billy patted Sean on the back.

"Leave him alone," said Stephenson.

"Yes ma'am. Hey, how come all your vehicles are black?" Billy shifted his gaze from the SUVs to the snowmobiles.

Stephenson looked at him. "Because they look cooler on TV."

Carroway started one of his snowmobiles, which made the air vibrate in a roar. Sean winced and pulled off a glove to reach into his parka. He pulled out a small cellophane pack with two yellow plugs, and tore it open with his teeth. He put one plug in each ear, slipping them under the ski cap.

"What're those?" Billy was looking at him.

"Shooter's ear plugs. Noise bothers me a lot more since..."

By the time he got his glove back on, he was chilled clear through. But now the noise of the revving snowmobile didn't bother him as much.

Carroway passed them their weapons. Sean looped his over his shoulder, where it weighed heavily on his back.

"Here," said Carroway, handing Sean a helmet.

"You're kidding, right?" Sean yelled above the engine noise.

"If you'd had one of these on last time..."

Sean decided not to argue. He tried to put on the helmet, which wouldn't fit over his ski cap. He removed the cap, and felt the cold bite his ears. The helmet now fit, and even more of the engine noise was muffled, for which Sean was grateful.

The helmet had a plastic visor to protect the face, and when Sean pulled it down, he felt like a questing knight. All he needed was a shield.

Sean worked the throttle, even though his hands felt separate from the rest of himself. The feeling of oddness within his own body was back, and strong now. The engine noise seeped into his head, despite the earplugs and helmet, and the throbbing at the base of his skull told him he would pay for it later with a massive headache. He settled into steering and shifting, letting his mind slip into a gray fog. He rode as an interloper in the vast wilderness.

Some time later, Carroway pulled up alongside and signaled Sean to stop. When Sean checked his watch, he was shocked to see it was already noon. The other snowmobiles were gathered in a bunch, and someone was passing out sandwiches.

Sean turned off his engine and took the Thermos cup of coffee Carroway handed him. He set the coffee on the seat and removed his helmet, replacing it with the ski cap.

His ears still buzzed from the engine drone, and they hurt where the helmet had squeezed them. He rubbed them with his gloved hands. His scarf was crusted with tiny balls of ice from the moisture exhaled by his breath. The scarf had begun to itch too much, so he unwound it and stuffed it in the back.

"Feel that pressure drop?" Carroway said. Sean looked up as the first few flakes of snow began to fall. "Storm's moving up fast. That limits us somewhat."

"Only if it gets bad," Stephenson said, alongside them.

"Oh, it'll get bad," Sean said, his mouth set in a grim line. "We need it, though. The Wendigo will come out in a storm, when nothing else will."

"Except damn fools like us," Carroway shook his head.

Sean's hands still felt clumsy, and he almost spilled his coffee. He quickly ate a sandwich and finished off the coffee, and handed the cup back to Carroway.

They all started off soon after, and rode through grasping branches to the crest of a hill.

"Where to?" Carroway gestured. There were two faint paths ahead, each forking in a different direction. "Which way to the Wendigo?"

Sean looked solemnly at each trail. "Right."

Carroway looked at him a moment and shrugged. "Right it is."

They roared down the hill. Sean felt a tingling, warming to the chase, feeling the ancient hunter within him rise.

The wind kicked up, and snow was falling now in earnest. Sean was straining to hear sounds other than the snowmobile and the wind. He thought he might have heard a high-pitched whine, and stopped to listen. He shut off the engine, and pulled off his helmet and removed the earplugs.

Exposed to the cold and the wind, he slowly turned from side to side like a radar dish, almost willing himself to hear something. He got nothing but the savage howl of the wind. Disappointed, he put his earplugs back in, put the helmet on, and switched on the engine once more.

Sean gave the group behind him a thumbs up signal, and they continued on. The trail led along a high ridge, with a line of evergreen trees on their right, forcing them to ride near the edge of a steep incline. Sean felt as if something was watching them, and tried to project his mind through the dense hedge of branches to see what lay behind them.

He came too close to the edge of the dropoff, and caught himself just in time. He accelerated to the bottom and turned to watch the others navigate the ridge. Carroway was followed by Russell, with the others making their way up the line of the ridge.

Sean was suddenly aware of immediate danger, and tried to yell out a warning. An unearthly cry rose over the sound of the wind, and Sean froze in terror. Something large and brown broke from the trees, and pushed Carroway's snowmobile over the edge, and Russell's as well.

Sean clawed at the strap holding the rifle case. He scooped it over his head, hearing the crackling of cold plastic and fiberglass. He unsnapped the catches of the case and pulled the Armalite free, but the Wendigo was no longer in sight.

Sean got off his machine and clumsily made his way through the drifts to where Carroway and Russell lay. Billy had reached them first, and several of Stephenson's team were coming toward them.

Billy was pumping Carroway's chest, performing CPR. He looked up at Sean. Strain showed on his face. "His heart."

"Keep going. What about him?" Sean indicated Russell, who lay in the snow.

"Machine rolled right over him, broke his leg."

"Where's Stephenson?"

"She took off after it."

"Damn." Sean gunned his engine and raced back up the ridge, following the track through the trees that Stephenson had made. He almost hit her machine, swerving just in time. She had bogged down in the thick snow, without a track to follow.

She waved him off before he tried to help her. "It went that way. Go! Go! Don't let it get away!"

Sean gunned his engine and did his best to maneuver between the trees. He came to a clearing, and saw the Wendigo on the other side. It turned to face him, only a few dozen meters away. It was covered with hair, but the features were all too familiar, disturbingly humanlike. The eyes showed intelligence, and seemed to beckon Sean, to draw him closer. They became whirling pools, like Poe's maelstrom, pulling in everything until there was no escape.

Crying out in anguish and release, Sean squeezed the trigger. There was a flat crack as the Armalite seemed to hiccup, and he saw a small puff where the bullet struck the Wendigo's shoulder. It screamed in pain, the sound ripping through Sean like a buzzsaw. He closed his eyes to shut it out, and when he opened them, the Wendigo was gone. He stared stupidly around, wondering if he had just had a hallucination.

Sean went to where the Wendigo had been. Scarlet splashes in the snow and large tracks confirmed the thing was real. Stephenson came buzzing up, wild and out of breath. She saw the bloody snow, and whooped in triumph.

At the far side of the clearing, the trees were too thick to get the snowmobile through. Sean swore mightily and got off, fighting his way through the branches. It was darker in the trees, and there was a stillness. He could easily follow the Wendigo's trail, with broken branches marking where the thing had crashed through. The snow was deep, and the going was hard, as Sean kept sinking. He thought it the perfect place for an ambush, and tried to remain alert. The thing was smart. The tracks led in a straight line, but was it clever enough to double back and lay a trap? Sean moved forward, weapon at the ready.

A gust of wind blew loose snow into one of the Wendigo's footprints, and Sean knew how little time there was before the storm obliterated the tracks. He wiped sweat from his lips with a bare hand, and realized with a shock he had left his glove behind. Cursing again, he moved on.

The tracks seemed to be closer together. Was the Wendigo tiring, or feeling the wound? Sean moved cautiously, shaking with anxiety. He heard a crack up ahead, and froze. He caught a glimpse of brown, but it was gone before he could get off a shot. He pushed on, gasping from the effort of breaching the snowdrifts.

He pushed aside another branch, and found himself in another clearing. And there it was, the creature of legend. It was stooped and bleeding, just a pitiful wounded animal, not a fearsome spirit. Sean smelled the strong, musty odor, and the memory of their previous encounter came flooding back.

Stephenson came up by his side, her breath ragged as she gulped for air. "Don't let it get away. Shoot it. *Shoot it.*"

Hands shaking, Sean raised the Armalite. The Wendigo looked at him, palms spread outward. It knew.

In his mind's eye, Sean targeted the neck with several rounds, then stitched bullets down to the chest. The Wendigo staggered, its mouth a rictus of pain, hands clutching the bloody head.

"Do it," Stephenson panted.

But Sean lowered the weapon. Stephenson shrieked and grabbed for the gun. Sean pushed her, and she fell back into the snow, sobbing.

The Wendigo turned and melted away into the trees. Sean watched it go, hoping it would live its life without being found again, although he doubted it. It was just a creature, not a demon. Knowing this, the whirlwind in Sean's mind had stopped. He was complete again, and had returned in full from the darkness where his mind had gone.

In the cold silence of the uncaring forest, the snow continued to fall.

THE END

AFTERWORD

If you were wondering why there are no cell phones or computers mentioned in this book, it's because it is set in a time before those items were commonplace. This was a tale begun long ago, in the mists of time. Many beginning writers want to write the Great American Novel. I wrote the Great Canadian Novel instead. But though it had compelling aspects, it was not told well. It took years of learning the craft before I was able to bring the tale to proper life. It is the first book I wrote, and it lay in it's horrible, fractured glory for many years, for unlike Mary Shelley, I didn't have the chops to make a go of it first time out.

But the idea is powerful, and kept calling over the years. Over the course of thirty-five years, I've worked to make this a tale worth telling. Bit by bit, I saw how to add tension and conflict to scenes that were nothing but talk, how to add characters that kicked the drama up, and how to make it entertaining and built in a much more satisfying way.

And if you feel like the ghost of Joseph Campbell haunts the pages, you'd be correct. Funny thing is, I wrote the story before I'd encountered Campbell's work, and was amazed that he so aptly described what was happening in Sean's journey. For this is the journey of the hero, who must travel to "the land of the dead" to bring back the specialized knowledge that allows him to properly take on the monster. We have various tropes of myth, such as the trickster god, the mentor, and many others. It is the intersection of ancient myth and legend and our more modern life, and Sean is the doorway between those worlds.

ABOUT THE AUTHOR

Dale T. Phillips has published novels, over 25 short stories and several story collections, poetry, and a non-fiction career book. He's appeared on stage, television, and in an independent feature film, *Throg*. He competed on *Jeopardy* and *Think Twice*. He's traveled to all 50 states, Mexico, Canada, and through Europe.

Connect Online:
Website: http://www.daletphillips.com
Blog: http://daletphillips@blogspot.com
Twitter: DalePhillips2

Other works by Dale T. Phillips

The Zack Taylor Mystery Series
A Memory of Grief
A Fall From Grace
A Shadow on the Wall

Story Collections
Apocalypse Tango (Sci-fi, End-of-world)
Fables and Fantasies (Fantasy)
Crooked Paths (Mystery/Crime)
Strange Tales (Magic Realism, Paranormal)
Halls of Horror (Horror)
Jumble Sale (Short Stories)

Non-fiction Career Help
How to Improve Your Interviewing Skills
For more information about the author and his works, go to:
http://www.daletphillips.com

Made in the USA
Middletown, DE
29 October 2023